IVAN AND THE DYNAMOS

Ivan and the Dynamos

Crystal Bowman

William B. Eerdmans Publishing Company
Grand Rapids, Michigan / Cambridge, U.K.

© 1997 Wm. B. Eerdmans Publishing Co.
255 Jefferson Ave. S.E., Grand Rapids, Michigan 49503 /
P.O. Box 163, Cambridge CB3 9PU U.K.

Printed in the United States of America

02 01 00 99 98 97   7 6 5 4 3 2 1

Library of Congress Cataloging-in-Publication Data

Bowman, Crystal.
Ivan and the dynamos / C.L. Bowman.
p.   cm.
Summary: Although eleven-year-old Andy is unhappy when
he does not get the hockey coach he wants, his new
coach uses a model approach to the team that brings
Andy one of the greatest experiences of his life.
ISBN 0-8028-5087-1 (cloth : alk. paper)
ISBN 0-8028-5090-1 (paper : alk. paper)
[1. Hockey — Fiction.]   I. Title.
PZ7.B68335Iv   1997
[Fic] — dc21   96-51150
CIP
AC

Though *Ivan and the Dynamos* is based on a
true story, the names have been changed, and
some of the events have been fictionalized.

Dedicated to Lou Rabaut,
for his love for children and his passion for hockey

With Special Thanks . . .

To the parents and players of the Dynamo hockey
team, whose commitment and enthusiasm
contributed to an unforgettable season.

To the Javoreks, for being the generous and
creative team sponsors.

To Steven Hayes, for faithfully recording the stats
and highlights of every game, and for editing
my hockey terminology.

To my editors, Amy Eerdmans De Vries
and Karen Klockner, whose insight and
expertise refined the manuscript and
brought it to completion.

To my husband and children, whose love and
support are a constant source of encouragement.

CONTENTS

CHAPTER ONE

Mom was on the telephone when I got home from school. I could tell she was talking about me, so I listened closely, hoping I could figure out what was going on.

"So Andy will be on your team? . . . Oh, I see. . . . Well, thanks for the call. We'll have him at practice Friday night. . . . Good-bye."

"So who was that?" I asked.

"That was Mr. Richards, your new hockey coach," she answered.

"Mr. Richards?" I said in disbelief. "I thought I was going to be on Coach Johnson's team!"

"You were, Andy," Mom explained calmly. "But Mr. Richards had two players on his team whose dads are sponsors. Since Coach Johnson's team didn't have a sponsor, you were traded onto Mr. Richards' team and one of those players was traded onto Coach Johnson's."

"Well, then," I replied, "I guess I'm not playin' hockey — 'cause I had Mr. Richards for practice last year and I don't like him."

My mom didn't say anything as I stormed up to my room, slammed the door, and flopped onto my bed.

1

I guess the best thing about my life right now is that it can't get much worse. We moved across town over the summer and I just started going to a new school. Being a sixth-grader at North Middle isn't much fun when you don't know anyone. Nobody talks to me in the halls, and lunch hour is the worst because I don't have anyone to sit with. Actually I do know one kid — Duffy Conners. He was on my hockey team last year. But his dad's the principal and everyone in the whole school knows him, so he probably couldn't care less that I go to his school.

I was really looking forward to playing hockey this year. I love ice skating more than anything else in the whole world. Being on a team last year was okay, but not as much fun as I thought it would be. I was a rookie and all the other kids were better than me. Sometimes they were jerks, especially when they scored goals and I didn't. The coach didn't let me play much, either. . . . What I couldn't figure out was how I was supposed to get better if I hardly got to play. But the league forms new teams every year, and there's this really neat coach, Mr. Johnson, who knows my dad and said he'd get me on his team. Now, if I can't play for Coach Johnson, I don't think I want to play.

My mom knocked on the door. "May I come in?"

"It's open," I mumbled.

"Honey, I know you're disappointed." Mom sat on my bed and put her arm around me. "But do you really think playing for Mr. Richards is going to be that bad? I've heard he's a good coach."

"I don't know," I sighed. "It's just that I really

wanted to play for Coach Johnson. "I figured if I was on his team, at least I'd get a chance to play."

"I know you like playing hockey," said my mom. "I'd hate to see you quit just because you didn't get on Mr. Johnson's team. Besides, if you don't play hockey, you're going to have to do something else."

"Why?" I asked knowing I was going to hear the same lecture I've heard at least a thousand times.

"You need to find something you enjoy," she answered, "and become good at it. Developing a skill helps you learn discipline and builds confidence."

"I know, I know," I groaned, knowing I shouldn't have brought it up.

"You know, Andy," Mom continued, "you don't *have* to do sports. You could take piano lessons from Aunt Karen or guitar lessons from Mr. Delos. I think you'd really enjoy music. Maybe you could become a famous rock star and people would stand in line for hours just to hear you."

"Oh, Mom!" I said with a laugh, "stop it!"

"Hey," she said as she brushed her hand through my hair, "I gotta go fix supper. You think it over for a while. I'll let you know when it's time to eat."

I turned over on my back and propped my head on my pillow as Mom left the room. I began to wonder if I'd ever be good at anything. Like James, for instance. He's my older brother. He's fourteen and loves playing tennis. He plays almost every day, which is the main reason we moved — our new house is much closer to the tennis club. James has so many trophies that my dad had to put extra shelves in his room. I glanced over at my shelf, which would be empty if it wasn't for my hat collection. Even my little sister Chrissy is good at stuff. She goes to gymnastics every week and gets all these ribbons and certificates. She's only eight years old, and she's the best softball player on her team. Last year she made two double plays and hit three home runs. I played baseball every spring for five years and never did anything like that.

"Let's eat!" I heard my mom calling from the kitchen.

I went downstairs and joined the family for dinner. After my dad said grace, we passed around the baked chicken, mashed potatoes, and glazed carrots.

"So what kind of day did everyone have?" asked my dad.

"I get to be student of the week," Chrissy announced proudly.

"It's because Anderson is at the beginning of the alphabet," I explained.

"Whatever the reason," commented my dad, "it's still an honor."

Then it was James's turn to brag.

"I talked to the tennis coach today," said James. "He said I could probably make the varsity team, even though I'm only a freshman."

"Well, I'm not surprised," replied my mom. "Nobody works harder at it than you do."

"And what kind of day did you have, Andy?" asked Dad.

"Oh, just great!" I answered sarcastically. "I sat

by myself again at lunch, and if I want to play hockey I have to be on Mr. Richards's team."

My dad stared at me for a minute as if he was trying to figure out what to say.

"Why don't you try making friends with Duffy Connors?" he suggested. "You already know him, and he's a nice kid."

I shrugged my shoulders and decided not to answer. My parents had no idea how hard it was being the new kid at school.

"Have you made your decision?" Mom asked as I helped clear the table. It was my night for dishes.

"I think I'll play hockey one more year," I answered. "But if I don't like being on Mr. Richards's team, I'm never going to play again."

"And then you'll become a rock star?" Mom teased.

"I guess so," I answered.

CHAPTER TWO

On Friday night my dad drove me to hockey practice. I looked out the window trying to ignore the songs on the radio. My dad was listening to 105.7 AM — his favorite oldies station. As far as I was concerned, all the songs sounded the same. Finally, I couldn't stand it any longer.

"Why do you listen to such dumb music?" I asked.

"What do you mean — dumb music?" Dad said defensively. "This is great music, and it's certainly better than that awful stuff you listen to. Heavy metal is nothing but noise, and rap was invented by someone who couldn't sing. All they do is mumble and spit. Anyone can do that!"

I couldn't help but laugh. My dad is pretty funny sometimes, and he's not bad for being an adult. But when he turned off the radio and got a serious look on his face, I braced myself. I knew it was lecture time.

"Andy I know you're bummed out about being traded," Dad began, "but at least give Mr. Richards a chance. He's supposed to be a good coach, from what I've heard."

I nodded and decided not to say anything, which

I've learned is sometimes the best thing to do. As we turned into the parking lot of the ice arena, I started to get nervous. I was excited to get back on the ice, but still had my doubts. Dad parked the van and said he'd get my equipment. The lights for the outdoor tennis courts went on suddenly, making it seem like three in the afternoon instead of seven o'clock at night. The tennis courts were next to the ice arena, and sometimes the hockey teams used them for what the coaches called "dry-land practice."

"This stuff weighs a ton!" complained Dad as he struggled with my hockey bag. "You better start lifting weights so you can carry your own equipment. I'm getting too old for this!"

"Well, Dad," I teased, "at least you don't have gray hair yet."

"Not yet," he said with a laugh, "but it won't be long."

As we walked through the double doors into the ice arena, the manager shouted, "Locker room number two for the Squirts."

The Squirts were the hockey players who were ten and eleven years old at the beginning of the season. This was my second year of being in the Squirt division 'cause I was eleven, going on twelve.

We were almost to the locker room when I saw Coach Johnson. His team had just finished practicing.

"Hey, there, Andy!" he said. "I'm awful sorry that you didn't get on my team. I did everything I could."

"I know," I told him. "Thanks for trying."

"Maybe next year," he added.

"Yeah," I agreed. "Maybe next year."

I opened the locker room door to join the rest of my teammates.

"See you later, Andy," said Dad as he left. "Have fun."

"Okay, Dad," I answered. "See you after practice."

"Hey, Andy!" said a familiar voice.

I looked across the locker room, and there stood Jamie Jones in his underwear. Jamie was on my team last year, and his dad was our sponsor.

"Hey, Jamie!" I said. "Is your dad sponsoring the team?"

"Yup," answered Jamie. "Looks like we're gonna be together again."

"Great!" I said as I went over and gave him a high five.

I really liked having Jamie's dad as a team sponsor. He was a big, huggable, friendly guy. He usually sat on the bench with us during games and told us how well we played, even when we didn't play well. Jamie's dad's name was Jack, and his mom's name was Janice, so they all had a first and last name that began with the letter J. Jamie has long blond hair that he wears in a ponytail during the games so that it doesn't blow in his face when he skates. Some of the referees think he's a girl, so they let him get away with things that the boys can't get away with. You see, there are a few girls who play hockey, but not enough to have their own league, so we have to let them play on the boys' teams if they want to play. I suppose it wouldn't be so bad having a girl on our team as long as she was good.

But I sure wouldn't want her to be in the locker room with us when we're all sitting around in our underwear.

Just then I heard the locker room door open, and in walked Mr. Richards and his son. Someone told me that his son was one of the best players in the league. I figured he was probably a jerk.

"Hey, guys!" said Mr. Richards, glancing around. "I'm glad you're all here. We're gonna take a few minutes to introduce ourselves, and then we'll be going outside for dry-land practice. I'm Coach Lou, and this is my son, Louie."

"Hi!" said Louie. "I'm Louie Richards. I'm in sixth grade, and I've been playing hockey for eight years."

Eight years! That meant he started playing hockey before he went to kindergarten. No wonder he was so good!

Next it was my turn, so I tried to say something important. "I'm Andy Anderson," I said. "This is my second year on a hockey team, and I like playing defense."

Whew! I was glad that was over.

Jamie was next. "My name is Jamie Jones," he said, "and I like getting penalties."

Everyone laughed at that remark, even Mr. Richards. Hockey players are usually proud when they get a penalty, because it makes them feel like they're tough. Sometimes, though, a penalty can really hurt the team, so it's important not to get one at the wrong time.

After all the players were introduced, we went out

9

to the tennis courts for dry-land practice. Everyone had a hockey stick, some golf balls, and a partner. I got paired up with a short kid who had red hair and freckles. He was the smallest guy on our team, but he seemed pretty good. His name was Mike Hanson. He was in the fifth grade, and he went to the same school as my sister. Mike and I passed the golf balls back and forth, but after a while it got boring.

"Hey," suggested Mike. "Why don't we try to hit each other with the balls?"

That sounded like more fun than passing the balls back and forth on the court, so I agreed. We were having a great time until I got hit in the leg. It hurt so bad that I didn't know whether to laugh or cry. Then Mr. Richards yelled at us for goofing off and made us pick up all the golf balls.

"I'm not against having fun," he explained to Mike and me, "but I don't want anyone getting hurt. Do you understand?"

Mike and I nodded as we picked up balls.

"Sorry," Mike whispered. "I didn't mean to get us in trouble."

"That's okay," I replied. "It was fun while it lasted."

From then on, Mike and I were buddies. I sort of felt like his big brother 'cause he seemed to look up to me.

Then it was time for real hockey practice — indoors, on the ice. My heart started pounding as I laced up my skates. There's nothing I love more than skating at full speed on a solid, smooth sheet of ice. I love getting all hot and sweaty and feeling the cold air sting my cheeks and forehead.

"Everyone can take nine or ten laps around the ice," announced Mr. Richards, "and then we're going to warm up the goalie."

We pushed and shoved our way onto the ice and began skating as fast as we could go. It was like a bunch of horses taking off at the beginning of a horse race. Most of us were able to keep up with each other, but soon Louie passed everyone and took the lead.

Mr. Richards blew his whistle. "Get your sticks," he hollered as he dumped a bucket of pucks on the ice. "It's time to give the goalie some exercise."

One after another, we shot the pucks toward the net, and one after another, the goalie stopped the pucks from going in.

"Wow!" I said to nobody in particular. "That guy's awesome!"

"He's supposed to be the best goalie in Squirts," said Louie. "That's why my dad wanted him on our team."

I was surprised when Louie answered me.

"I think he goes to my school," I said.

"His name's Jimmy Cleaver," said Louie. "He goes to North Middle."

"Yep, that's where I go," I said. "But this is my first year there, so I don't know many of the kids."

"I go to the Zoo School," Louie told me.

"The Zoo School?" I repeated in surprise. "I've heard some things about the Zoo School, but I've never met anyone who went there. Is it fun?"

"It's great!" Louie exclaimed. "You get to spend a lot of time outdoors with the animals. It's much better than boring classroom school."

"Well," I agreed, "anything would be better than boring classroom school."

I didn't say this to Louie, but I'm not sure I'd like going to the Zoo School and being with animals every day. It certainly wouldn't be good for my allergies.

Mr. Richards blew his whistle again. "Time for drills," he shouted. "Tonight we're going to work on passing, and next week we'll learn one-on-one tactics as well as team tactics."

We paired up and passed pucks back and forth across the ice. Even though I hate drills, it sure felt good to be on the ice with a hockey stick in my hand. Finally practice was over, and we all headed for the locker room. While we were getting out of our hockey gear, Mr. Richards said he wanted to talk to us about something important.

"Mr. Jones and I have decided that it would be fun to pretend we're a Russian hockey team," he said. "We all know that the Russians are the best hockey players in the world. By having the image of a Russian team, we could put fear into our opponents! Our team is going to be called the Dynamos. Dynamo is short for 'dynamoelectric machine,' which means a forceful, energetic individual. Everyone will need to choose a Russian name from the list I'm going to pass around. Next Friday I'll ask for your Russian names, and we'll have them printed on the backs of your jerseys. Our team logo, a lightning bolt, will be printed on the front along with the team name. Now, unless anyone has questions, you're dismissed. We'll see you one week from tonight."

The whole team started talking at once. Everyone was grabbing the list and trying to look at the Russian names. Just then my dad walked into the locker room.

"It smells like you had a good practice," he joked.

Jamie laughed. "What do you expect a hockey locker room to smell like — a perfume store?"

"I think I'd rather be in a perfume store right now," said Dad as he picked up the sheet of paper from the bench. "Hey, what's this?"

"It's a list of Russian names." I explained. "We're going to be a Russian team, so we all need to pick a Russian name."

"Hmmm," said Dad as he examined the list. "These are pretty difficult names. I'm not sure I can pronounce half of them. You'd better pick one that you can spell."

"Good thinkin'!" I agreed. "How about Ivan? I can spell that one."

"Ivan, the Terrible," said Dad. "Good choice."

I put a check by IVAN so my teammates would know it was taken.

Then I zipped up my hockey bag, and Dad and I headed for the van.

"So how was practice?" he asked.

"It was okay," I answered. "But I still wish I had Coach Johnson."

"Well," remarked Dad trying to look on the bright side, "being a Russian team should be fun."

"I hope so," I answered. "It might be fun as long as the other teams don't think it's stupid."

"The other teams will be sorry they didn't think of it first," Dad suggested.

I hoped my dad was right.

CHAPTER THREE

I rolled over in bed to check the time on my alarm clock. I thought for sure it was the middle of the night. I squinted at the bright red numerals and realized it was seven forty-five, time to get up and get ready for church. I noticed that the hall lights were on, and I overheard my mom yelling at Chrissy for stuffing all her dolls and animals into her closet. Chrissy couldn't find her shoes, and Mom was in a panic because we might be late for church.

"Do we have a problem here?" I asked as I stuck my head into Chrissy's room.

"Oh, be quiet!" shouted Chrissy. "And get out of my room!"

"But I'm not *in* your room," I pointed out.

"Well your head is!" shouted Chrissy, "Now get out!"

Then Mom chimed in, "If you would like to help Chrissy find her shoes, that would be fine. Otherwise please leave her alone."

"Oh, I'll help her," I grumbled.

"Thank you," replied Mom in a not so thankful voice. "I have plenty of other things to do right now."

15

"Maybe if you weren't such a slob," I suggested to Chrissy, "you wouldn't lose all your stuff."

"Well, you're not so perfect yourself," she said defensively.

I searched for Chrissy's shoes under her bed, in her closet, behind the dressers, and even in the waste basket, but they were nowhere to be found.

"Here's a *Boxcar* book," I said as I tossed it to her.

"Oh, good!" said Chrissy as she stuffed it into her purse. "I've been looking for that."

"I give up," I sighed. "This could take the rest of my life."

"Oh, look! I found a shoe!" Chrissy shouted, as though she had just discovered America.

"Well, hallelujah!" I replied. "But one shoe isn't going to be of much use unless you find the other one."

"Well, you haven't been much help!" retorted Chrissy.

"Fine," I snapped as I left her room, "find the other one yourself!"

When I went into the kitchen to eat breakfast, I noticed the empty milk bottle on the table next to James.

"Thanks for hoggin' all the milk," I said. "What am I supposed to put on my cereal, orange juice?"

"If you wanna put orange juice on your cereal, no one's gonna stop you." James replied. "Or you could get the other bottle of milk from the refrigerator."

"Why didn't you tell me we had more milk?" I asked.

"I just did," answered James as he got up from his chair and brought his dishes to the sink.

I decided to ignore James, eat my breakfast, and get ready for church. Then I joined the rest my family in the driveway, where Dad was ready and waiting. Chrissy somehow managed to find her other shoe, and I must admit she looked pretty cute in her Sunday dress. When we got to church, we marched our way down the aisle to the second row from the front. We always sit close to the front because my mom thinks we listen better when we're close to the action.

While the offering was being taken I started thinking about hockey. I wondered if the other players had chosen their Russian names yet, and I wondered if I'd like having Mr. Richards for a coach. I thought about how great it would be if we were ever the Squirt champions. I pictured our team on the ice with Mr. Richards holding up the first place trophy. Then I stopped daydreaming for a minute and looked over at Chrissy, who was reading her *Boxcar Children* book.

"Put it away," Mom whispered. "It's time to listen."

Sometimes it's hard for me to listen to the sermon, but not today. It seemed like our pastor was talking right to me.

"Things don't always go the way we want them to," he said. "Disappointment is a part of life. But we have to believe that God knows what's best for us. He will always help us through the hard times."

I guess I already knew those things from my parents, but it was good to hear my pastor talk about it today. After the sermon, we sang the doxology, and then church was over. Mom and Dad chatted with friends on their way out of church, while James, Chrissy, and I tried to figure out a quick escape through the clusters of people. The bad thing about sitting in the front is that we're always the last to get out. If there was ever a fire in church, we would die for sure.

On Sunday afternoon I decided to work on my leaf collection for science class. I called Duffy Conners to see if he wanted to collect leaves with me since he was in my science class. I figured he might have someone else to work with, or maybe he was already finished, but I gave it a shot anyway.

"Hello, Duffy?" I said. "This is Andy Anderson. I was wondering if you've collected leaves for the science project yet."

"Some," he answered. "But I still need a few more. Crown Lake has some good trees. I'll meet ya there at two o'clock."

"Okay, see ya," I replied.

Just before two, I hopped on my bike and headed for the lake, which was only a few blocks away. When I got there, Duffy was already picking leaves and stuffing them into his bag.

"Hey, Duffy," I asked, "how many more leaves do you need?"

"About ten more," he answered. "How about you?"

"I need about a half dozen," I replied. "So what do you think of this project?"

"I think it's pretty dumb," he said. "Like it's really

going to make a difference twenty years from now if we know how to identify a few leaves."

Then Duffy began speaking in a high voice, imitating Ms. Bowens. He was so funny I couldn't help but laugh.

"Oh, yes, this one is a maple, and this is an oak. And I think that one over there is a dogwood, and this one looks like a blue spruce, and the one that makes you itch is poison ivy."

"Uh, Duffy," I interrupted, "I don't think poison ivy is a tree."

"Well, it has leaves, doesn't it?" defended Duffy in his normal voice. "Besides, if I put a poison ivy leaf in my collection, maybe Ms. Bowens will touch it and break out in a rash. And then she won't be able to come to school for a week, and we can torture the substitute teacher!"

"Sounds like a good plan," I said, "if it doesn't get you expelled from school."

"I can't get expelled," Duffy said with a laugh. "My dad's the principal."

After an hour of gathering leaves, we both decided we had more than enough. Collecting the leaves was the easy part. Figuring out what kind of leaves they were was going to be the challenge. As we walked along the edge of the lake, Duffy picked up some smooth stones and began skimming them across the surface of the water.

"You playin' hockey this year?" asked Duffy.

"Yeah," I answered as my own stone skipped three times before sinking. "I didn't get the coach I wanted, but I'm on a team called the Dynamos. We're supposed to be like a Russian team."

"That sounds pretty neat," Duffy replied. "I'm on Ben's Auto Shop this year. We have a good coach but our jerseys are ugly. Got any good players?"

"Louie Richards is good," I answered, "and I think our goalie is pretty good. But I don't know about the rest of the guys. Too bad we're not on the same team again."

"Yeah," said Duffy. "I hope I don't hurt you when I knock you down."

I laughed as though I knew he was kidding, but I wasn't sure he was.

"Well, I gotta get going," Duffy said. "See ya tomorrow."

"Yeah," I answered, "See ya tomorrow."

CHAPTER FOUR

On Monday at lunch I saw Jimmy Cleaver in the cafeteria. I didn't know if I should say anything — I wasn't even sure if he knew who I was. But I decided to give it a try.

"Hey, Jimmy!" I said, "How's it going?"

"Hi," said Jimmy as he looked me over. "Hey, aren't you on my hockey team?"

"Yeah," I answered, relieved that he recognized me. "My name's Andy."

"Have a seat," Jimmy said. "So where you from?"

"Well," I explained, "we used to live across town, but my parents wanted to be closer to the tennis club where my brother plays, so we moved here during the summer."

"Well, you're at the right place," Jimmy remarked. "North Middle has a lot of hockey players and even a teacher who plays hockey."

"Really?" I asked in disbelief.

"Really," answered Jimmy. "Don't you have Mr. Fisher for English?"

"Yeah," I said wondering what Mr. Fisher had to do with our conversation.

"Well," explained Jimmy, "Mr. Fisher played

hockey in college. He's a good goalie, and he's a friend of Mr. Richards."

"So?" I asked still wondering what Jimmy was getting at.

"So he's going to help Mr. Richards with our team, but he'll mostly be coaching me."

I couldn't believe what I was hearing! My English teacher would be at all my practices and games? I wasn't sure if that was good or bad.

"Isn't it kind of weird having a teacher for a coach?" I asked Jimmy.

"He was my coach last year, too," explained Jimmy, "so I think of him more as a coach than a teacher. I know it seems weird, but you'll get used to it."

At that moment, the bell rang and everyone scrambled to clean up wrappers, gather books, and move on to fifth hour — science class for me. I grabbed a seat next to Duffy and listened to Ms. Bowens remind us about our leaf collections.

"Leaf collections are due next week," she announced. "I hope none of you has waited until the last minute."

Duffy and I exchanged glances and rolled our eyes. We both had enough leaves, but we hadn't even started on the identifying part. I had collected a few extra leaves, just to be on the safe side.

"Hey, Jason," I whispered to Jason Potts, who never did his homework on time, "how are you doing on the project?"

"No problem!" answered Jason. "My dad's taking

me to Fred's Nursery today. They've got hundreds of trees, and they're all labeled. It'll be a piece of cake!"

I had never thought of going to a nursery to get leaves. I wasn't sure if it was a great idea, or if it was cheating. At any rate, I had all the leaves I needed. All I had to do now was figure out what kind they were.

Music class followed science, and then I had gym. It was a warm day, so we had gym outdoors. I like outdoor gym much better than indoor gym, where everyone gets so hot and sweaty.

Today we were playing soccer. I don't play much soccer, but it's a lot like hockey except you use a ball instead of a puck. The score was three to five. All of a sudden one of the players accidentally kicked the ball into Crown Lake. I ran after the ball, and without giving it a second thought, I went into the lake to retrieve the soccer ball. All the kids jumped up and down and cheered, and the teacher thanked me for saving the ball. From then on, everyone in my gym class knew who I was.

The rest of the week went by quickly, and soon it was Friday evening. After two tacos and a glass of lemonade, I was on my way to hockey practice. I wasn't as nervous as I was the week before, but I still wondered what this practice would be like. I didn't want do anything more to upset Mr. Richards. I looked over at my dad, who was tapping his fingers on the steering wheel in rhythm to the Beach Boys.

"Am I gonna have to listen to oldies every time I go to practice?" I asked.

"If you're ridin' with me you will," Dad answered.

"Well I guess it's better than walking," I sighed as we approached the arena.

Dad dropped me off at the door, and I went straight to the locker room. Dad had decided that I should carry my own equipment. Within a few minutes all the players were there getting dressed. While we were putting on our hockey stuff, Mr. Richards announced that he had a few things to say.

"Every player will be given a playbook this evening," he explained. "I expect you to read it, study it, and learn it. The book explains everything from rules and terms to plays and strategies. If you study the plays, you'll understand my instructions."

I sort of liked the idea of having a playbook. That way I didn't have to learn everything the hard way. This was one kind of homework I wouldn't mind doing.

"A few more things," added Mr. Richards. "I don't want anyone whining to me about not getting enough playing time during a game. I don't care if you're a rookie or if you've been playing since you were in diapers. If you play hard and do what I tell you to do, you'll have so much time on the ice you'll be begging me to take you off!"

"All right!" exclaimed Jamie Jones. "This sounds like my kind of hockey."

"Getting penalties is your kind of hockey," teased Louie.

"Hey, listen up, guys!" continued Mr. Richards. "I'm almost finished. There's one thing I won't tolerate on this team, and that's the criticism of other players.

We win together and we lose together. There is no 'I' in team. We all make mistakes from time to time. When you make a mistake, you'll be thankful for this rule. Now go out there and have a good practice."

I was one of the first players out of the locker room and onto the ice. We skated several laps around the rink, and then we worked on team tactics. I listen closely to Mr. Richards as he told us what to do. He sure seemed to know a lot about hockey.

"In team tactics," explained Mr. Richards, "we will use two or more players to accomplish a goal. That's why it's important for you to be in the correct position and be able to anticipate what your teammate is going to do."

I liked the idea of having plays and strategies. Being able to outsmart the other team is just as important as being able to outskate them. I began to realize that playing hockey was more than moving the puck toward the goal, and that I'd have to pay attention to every detail of the game.

Hockey practice was really hard. I tried my best to keep up with everyone else, but so many of the guys seemed to know more than I did. I wished that I had started playing hockey when I was younger so I'd be one of the better players. I decided that I'd just have to work extra hard to keep up.

It was pretty quiet in the locker room after practice, I guess because everyone was so tired.

"Before you guys take off," announced Mr. Richards, "I want you to write your name next to a Russian name on this list. I will be calling you by your Russian name throughout the season, and you may call me Coach Lou. Next week you'll meet Mr. Fisher, our goalie coach."

"Shouldn't we call you Coach Dynamo?" asked Mike Hanson.

"We're all Dynamos," laughed Mr. Richards. "You'd better stick with Coach Lou so I know who you're talkin' to."

When everyone chose his Russian name, I asked Mr. Richards if I could see the list.

"You may see it if you're willing to read it," answered Mr. Richards.

"Okay," I answered. "I'll give it a try."

"Ya have to stand up on the bench," instructed Louie.

I stood up on the bench, cleared my throat, and in my best announcer's voice read the names out loud while everyone listened.

"Benny Baker is Sergei," I announced. "Andy Anderson, yours truly, is Ivan. Ricky Clay is Igor."

"Igor the monster!" remarked Mike Hanson.

"Jimmy Cleaver, our goalie, is Tretyak," I continued. "Kurt Hall chose Vladimir, and Mike Hanson is Petr. Jamie Jones is Boris, and Mark Olson picked the name Victor."

I stopped reading for a second and took the list to Mr. Richards.

"Who's this kid?" I asked as I pointed to a name.

"That's Freddie Rogers," explained Mr. Richards. "He's on our team but he won't be here for a while because he's having his tonsils out."

26

"Get on with the names!" shouted Jamie.

"Billy Peterson chose the name Mikail," I continued, "and Louie picked the name Vyacheslav."

"We better just call him Chevy," said Jamie.

"Good idea," added Mr. Richards.

"The last name on the list is Denny Smith," I announced. "Denny chose the name Alexi."

"So there ya have it," exclaimed Mr. Richards. "These will be our names for the season."

"I can't even remember everyone's real name," said Jamie. "How am I going to remember all the Russian names?"

"Forget the real names," suggested Mike. "All we need to learn are the Russian names."

"Okay, Petr," said Jamie. "See ya next week."

"Yeah, see ya, Boris," answered Mike with a laugh.

Mr. Jones came in the locker room to tell Jamie to hurry up. "Hey, Andy," he said, "I'm glad you're on our team this year. Mr. Richards is a good coach. You'll learn a lot."

"I hope so!" I answered.

CHAPTER FIVE

I was glad we had one more practice before our first game on Saturday. I was beginning to get pretty nervous. At least we had a few first-year players on our team — so I probably wouldn't be the *worst* one. As far as I'm concerned, there's nothing more awful than being the worst player on a team!

I liked seeing Jimmy Cleaver at school every day. I usually sat with him at lunch, and he called me Ivan instead of Andy, which made me feel like a professional hockey player. Every time I was in English class, I wanted to tell Mr. Fisher that I was on the hockey team. But he never mentioned it to me, so I figured he didn't know. I decided to wait until Friday night when he'd eventually figure it out.

In science class, I was happy to discover that I got an A on my leaf collection. Ms. Bowens said that I did an exceptional job. I was embarrassed when she announced it in front of the whole class, but I wasn't nearly as embarrassed as Jason Potts, who got an F because he cheated. Ms. Bowens was very upset when she found out that all of his leaves came from Fred's Nursery.

"That was not what I intended when I gave out

the assignment!" she exclaimed. "No one gets away with shortcuts in my class!"

"Good job, Andy," whispered Duffy, who was sitting behind me.

"Thanks," I whispered back. "What did you get?"

"I got an A, too," he answered.

I gave him the thumbs-up and tried to stay awake for the rest of science class.

The week seemed more like a month, but finally it was Friday night, and I was on my way to practice again. Mrs. Cleaver offered to pick me up, and from that night on Jimmy and I carpooled to practice. At least Mrs. Cleaver didn't listen to the oldies station.

When we got to practice, Mr. Fisher and Mr. Richards were in the locker room discussing their plans for the evening.

"Well," said Mr. Fisher as he looked at Jimmy and me. "There's a couple familiar faces. Haven't I seen you somewhere before?"

"Only every day at school," laughed Jimmy.

"Hey, Andy," asked Mr. Fisher, "why didn't you tell me you were on the team? You're not afraid of me, are ya?"

I shrugged my shoulders and wasn't sure what to say. It seemed strange having my English teacher in the locker room.

"I didn't know if I should talk about hockey at school," I told him.

"Are you kiddin'?" he exclaimed. "The more hockey talk at school, the better!"

Mr. Fisher got a strange look on his face as he examined the list of players.

"What do we have here?" he asked. "A bunch of exchange students from Russia?"

Mr. Richards laughed as he explained, "Oh, I forgot to tell you that the kids all chose Russian names."

"Do I need to know how to spell them or just pronounce them?" asked Mr. Fisher.

"Let's start with pronouncing them," answered Mr. Richards. "The kids will be responsible for the spelling."

"Why do you think I picked the name Ivan?" I asked.

"Smart thinkin'," said Mr. Fisher. "I think I can handle that one. It's the other names I'm worried about!"

Soon everyone was dressed and ready for practice. We warmed up by skating laps, and then we worked on passing and shooting. After that, we rehearsed plays, positioning, and one-on-one defense. Louie, Benny, and Kurt practiced face-offs with Mr. Richards, since they would be playing center most of the time. I was going to be playing defense, but that was okay with me. At least I'd be on the ice this year, instead of sitting on the bench.

"We have one more item on our agenda for this evening," Mr. Richards announced when we were back in the locker room. "We need to choose our captains. On Russian teams, they have three co-captains. The co-captains are identified by having the letter *K* on their jerseys. We will be selecting three players to be the captains this year, and I think we should allow some likely candidates to give a brief speech before we take a vote."

I was interested in being a co-captain, but I sure didn't have a speech prepared. Louie Richards stood right up on the bench and began his speech: "I think I should be voted captain because I have eight years of experience. I am a team player and will promise at all times to do what is best for the team."

The boys began to support Louie with rousing cheers and whistles until Mr. Richards quieted them down. I was surprised when Mike Hanson stood up next.

"I think I should be a captain," he said confidently, "because I never give up and I'm as tough as anyone twice my size!"

When Mike sat down, Kurt Hall jumped up to put in his bid for the title. "I can lead this team to victory!" he proclaimed. "Vote for me and you will not be disappointed!"

My dad walked into the locker room as Mr. Richards asked for more volunteers.

"I'd like to be a captain," I said, not knowing what to say next.

Before I could finish, Jamie chimed in, "If you vote for me, I'll make sure we get good snacks."

When everyone started laughing, Mr. Richards said he'd heard enough speeches and that it was time to vote. I knew my dad was anxious to leave, so I cast my ballot and decided not to hang around for the results.

"What was that all about?" Dad asked as we left the arena.

"Mr. Richards was giving the guys a chance to run for captain of the team," I answered.

"I see," said Dad. "So who do you think will get the honors?"

"Well," I explained, "there's going to be three co-captains. Louie will probably be one of them. He's the best player on the team, and I think he deserves it."

"You're right, Andy," said Dad. "And I'm glad you feel that way instead of being jealous."

"I'm not jealous of anyone," I explained. "I just hate it when the good players act like jerks. I thought Louie would be a jerk 'cause he's so good. But so far he's been pretty nice."

"And what do you think of your coach?" asked Dad.

"I don't know," I answered. "He knows a lot about hockey, but I hope he doesn't yell at us during the games."

When we got home I took a shower, ate a plate of spaghetti, and went to bed. I thought I would be too nervous to sleep, but instead I was too tired to stay awake. I set my alarm for seven o'clock. Tomorrow would be my first game with the Dynamos.

•   •   •

I woke up at six in the morning. I tried to go back to sleep, but I couldn't. In two more hours I'd be in the locker room getting ready for the game. Would I remember all the things I had learned in practice? Would I know where my positions were and what to do with the puck if I got it? I was glad I was going to play defense. I probably wouldn't have a chance to score a goal, but that was okay with me. I just hoped that I'd play well and not mess up.

When I got out of bed and went downstairs, I was surprised to find my mom already up.

"You'd better eat a healthy breakfast this morning," she said. "No junk food for hockey players."

"I'm not hungry," I replied.

"Too excited to eat?" asked Mom.

"Guess so," I answered.

Just then my dad came in with the morning paper.

"Well, aren't we up bright and early?" he said.

"I couldn't sleep," I explained.

"Butterflies?" he teased.

"Probably," I answered.

"Well there's nothing like a good hot breakfast to tame those butterflies," Dad said. "Why don't you get your jacket, and I'll take you out for pancakes."

I like going out for breakfast with my dad, especially when we go by ourselves. My dad lets me choose the restaurant and order whatever I want. I grabbed my jacket and jumped in the car.

"So where do you want to go?" asked Dad.

"How about the Pancake House?" I suggested.

"The Pancake House it is," he replied.

When we got to the restaurant, I ordered blueberry pancakes, a glass of orange juice, and a side order of bacon. My dad ordered a glass of apple juice and a bagel. He never eats very much for breakfast, so I knew he had taken me out just to spend time together before the game.

"So what do you think, Ivan," he asked. "Are the Dynamos any good?"

I shrugged my shoulders. "I think we're pretty good, but I won't know until we play a real game. I'll be playing defense today."

"Defense is important," commented Dad.

"I know," I agreed, "but you don't get a chance to score."

"There's a lot more to hockey than scoring goals," Dad said.

I nodded my head and ate my pancakes. When we were done eating, the waitress came by and handed the bill to my dad.

"I believe that goes to the young man," Dad said, nodding toward me.

"Oh, excuse me," she replied as she gave the bill to me. "Treating your old man to breakfast, son?"

"Yes, Ma'am," I replied.

"Well, I hope you're a big tipper," she said with a wink.

When the waitress left, my dad handed me twenty dollars and let me take the bill and the money up to the cash register. I like it when my dad lets me pay the bill. He's always impressed when I come back with the correct change.

We stopped home to pick up my hockey equipment. Mom, James, and Chrissy were dressed and ready to go. They were all coming to my first game of the season. I knew Mom and Dad wanted to see me play, but I figured James and Chrissy were coming along because Mom made them.

Everyone was quiet on the way. I didn't know if it was because they were all tired or if they were afraid to say anything. I was relieved when my mom finally broke the silence.

"I hope you have a good game, Andy," she said. "The first game of the season is always tough because you're not used to playing together."

I nodded in agreement.

"Who are you playing?" asked James.

"Ben's Auto Shop," I answered. "Duffy Conners is on that team."

"The Dynamos sure have a cool name for their team," remarked James. "That was nice of Mr. Jones to let you use the name Dynamos instead of his company's name."

"I know," I agreed. "If we weren't the Dynamos we would have been Jones's Lumber Company. At least 'Dynamos' sounds like a real hockey team instead of an advertisement."

"Just think if you had a sponsor that owned a diaper company," remarked Chrissy. "Then your team name would be 'Soft and Dry Diapers' or 'Better Bottoms'!"

We all laughed at Chrissy's team names and came up with a few of our own.

Finally, we arrived at the ice arena. This was the moment I had been waiting for. There was no more time to practice drills or learn new plays. It was time to play hockey.

CHAPTER SIX

It was really noisy in the locker room. Everyone was talking at once except for Louie, who was studying the playbook.

"Are ya nervous?" Louie asked when I sat on the bench next to him to tie my skates.

"A little, I guess. It's been six months since I've played a real game." Actually, I was more than a little nervous. I was terrified.

"No matter how often I play, I still get nervous," confessed Louie.

"But you're so good," I reminded him. "Why would you be nervous?"

"Because everyone expects me to do everything right and score goals when we get behind. If I don't play better than everyone else, I feel like I've let the team down."

First of all, I couldn't believe that a kid like Louie would ever be nervous. And second of all, I never thought about what it must be like for everyone to expect you to be the best. I guess being a rookie wasn't so bad after all. At least people didn't expect much.

"A quick announcement before we go out," interrupted Mr. Richards in an attempt to get everyone's attention. "The co-captains for the season are going to be Louie Richards, Kurt Hall, and Jamie Jones. We congratulate you and will look up to you as our team leaders."

I got a lump in my throat as Mr. Richards gave each of them a red *K* and told them to have the letters sewn on their jerseys before our next game. I guess I didn't really expect anyone to have voted for me.

"Two minutes and we're on the ice," instructed Mr. Richards. "Be sure your skates are tight and your mouth guards are in place. Keep your heads up and listen closely to me and Mr. Fisher. Mr. Jones will be on the players' bench. He'll tell you when it's your turn to get on and off the ice. Play hard, be tough, and most of all, have fun!"

"Let's go!" shouted Louie as he led our team onto the ice. The other team was already warming up. When I saw Ben's Auto Shop printed on their jerseys, I was glad I was a Dynamo. Our lightning bolt was especially cool.

"Hey, what's with the names?" I overheard one of the referees ask Mr. Richards. "I thought these kids were from around here!"

"The Dynamos are from Russia," was all Mr. Richards said.

The confused referee skated to the center of the rink while Mr. Richards sat on the bench and smiled.

The buzzer sounded. The starting players took their positions on the ice while the rest of us went to the bench. I knew it'd only be a few short minutes until I'd be out on the ice having my chance to defend the puck. Louie won the face-off, and in less than a minute our team was in the offensive zone making Ben's Auto Shop wish they had some spare parts. The players passed the puck back and forth until Louie took a shot and scored.

"Way to go Louie!" shouted Mike and Jamie from the bench. The players who were on the ice slapped Louie on the back as they made their way to the bench.

"Ivan, you're on!" shouted Mr. Jones.

My heart started beating so fast I could feel it pounding in my ears. I skated to my position on the ice and waited for the face-off. Benny Baker was playing center. He won the face-off for the Dynamos, but the puck was soon taken away by the other team. Both teams quickly shifted to our defensive zone. I think I skated faster than I ever did in my whole life.

Ben's Auto tried to score, but Jimmy's goal-tending was more than they could handle. Then Benny got control of the puck and headed back to our offensive zone. Everything was happening so fast, but I somehow managed to keep up. I had forgotten all about being nervous and was so hot I could feel sweat dripping off my forehead.

All of a sudden, a player right next to me stole the puck from Benny. I was so mad, I went after him and got the puck back. I passed it to Benny. Benny passed it to Mark Olson. Mark shot the puck and scored! We all went nuts. The rest of the team jumped off the bench and mobbed us on the ice.

"Let's get on with the game, boys," shouted the referee as he broke up our celebration.

"Whew!" I was thankful I had a chance to rest. I was exhausted!

"Nice playin', Ivan," said Mr. Jones as he passed me a water bottle.

"Thanks," I muttered between sips. I felt like hugging Mr. Jones right then, but I decided to save it for the locker room.

Jamie Jones was on the ice now with Ricky Clay, Kurt Hall, Mike Hanson, and Billy Peterson. I thought that Ricky and Billy were playing pretty good for being rookies, but it was Mike that really had my attention. He weaved in and out of the other players so fast that no one could keep up with him. It seemed as though being small for him was an advantage.

As I gazed across the ice and looked at the people in the stands, I saw Mom, Dad, James, and Chrissy sitting with the other players' families. I was glad my whole family was there. I was surprised they were cheering and whistling so much. They acted like it was an important game or something.

"Line change," shouted Mr. Jones.

I couldn't believe I was back on the ice already. I'd barely had a chance to catch my breath. Ben's Auto Shop started playing tougher. I could feel the tension in the air. The game seemed to be going faster and faster, as if somehow it was gaining momentum — like a steel ball rolling down a mountainside. All of a sudden, Duffy Conners scored a goal for Ben's Auto Shop. Then before we could figure out what happened, another player for Ben's Auto Shop scored a goal and tied the game!

We were speechless as Mr. Richards summoned us to the bench.

"Don't let the tie shake your confidence," he instructed. "It's early in the game. These guys are tough, but we're tougher. Get out there, play hard, and show the world what Dynamos are made of!"

I was back on the ice with Louie, Mark, Ricky, and Denny Smith. The puck was passed back and forth as we skated from one side of the rink to the other. I didn't like the way one of the players ran into me, so I gave him a shove and knocked him down on the ice. When I heard the referee's whistle, I knew I was in trouble.

"Two minutes for roughing!" shouted the referee. "Dynamo Number 91!"

I couldn't believe it! How could I be the first player on our team to get a penalty? As I followed the referee to the penalty box, I wondered if Mr. Richards was going to be mad. Everyone was shouting and screaming, but I couldn't tell what anyone was saying because it all blended together in one huge roar.

I glanced over at Mr. Richards. He was watching the game and didn't seem to be too concerned about my penalty. I leaned over just far enough out of the penalty box to catch Mr. Jones's eye. He nodded and grinned, and I felt much better. Then I just fell back against the wall and rested while I served my penalty.

When my two minutes expired, we were back at full strength. I was thankful that Ben's Auto didn't score while we were shorthanded. Louie somehow got possession of the puck and outskated everyone for a clean breakaway, which resulted in another goal for the Dynamos. With a score of three to two, we were back on top. Unfortunately, Ben's Auto Shop didn't give up and quickly came back to tie the score once again.

The sound of the buzzer meant the end of the first period and a brief break for the players. After a few words of encouragement, Mr. Richards sent us back on the ice for the second period. Both teams played more defensively, which made it harder to score. I had two more take-aways and a pass to Kurt Hall, who shot and scored near the end of the second period. At the beginning of the third period, we were once again leading with a score of four to three. Louie managed another breakaway and scored his third goal, which made the score five to three. Three goals meant a hat trick for Louie. I couldn't believe that anyone could get a hat trick in his very first game of the season!

Ben's Auto Shop didn't give up. It seemed as though they played better when they were behind. They managed to put in two more goals. The score was now tied at five each. I looked at the time clock on the wall. There were only three minutes left in the game — enough time for either team to score. I hoped the game wouldn't end in a tie. That would be really boring!

I was out on the ice again and knew it was my last opportunity to help the team. Getting a penalty now would be a big mistake, so I was careful to play by the rules. Jamie and I were playing defense and doing a pretty good job of keeping the puck in our offensive zone. With two minutes left in the game,

Jamie made a beautiful pass to Kurt, who shot and scored! We were all going crazy until Mr. Richards called us to the bench.

"We haven't won yet!" he reminded us. "The other team can still score!"

Mr. Richards sent out a strong line, using our best players for the final two minutes of the game. Kurt, Louie, Benny, Jamie, and Mark took their positions on the ice and prepared for what turned out to be the last face-off of the game.

Ben's Auto Shop won the face-off, but Mark took the puck away and passed it to Kurt. The Dynamos kept control of the puck as the seconds ticked away on the clock. I was so excited I kept moving my head back and forth so I could watch the game and the clock at the same time.

Five, four, three, two, one — the buzzer sounded! The game was over. The Dynamos had won! I jumped over the wall with the other players to join our team on the ice. We all hugged each other while sticks and gloves went flying. The coaches came out on the ice and congratulated the Dynamos. Then we formed a line to shake hands with our opponents. The players for Ben's Auto Shop were good sports.

"Good game, Andy," said Duffy as we passed each other in the lineup.

"Good game," I said.

"We'll get ya next time," added Duffy.

"We'll see," I answered, as I headed for the locker room.

When I walked into the locker room, Mr. Jones

was standing there with a big smile on his face, staring straight at me.

"You played out of your mind!" he exclaimed. "Did you spend the summer in Canada or something?"

"No, I spent it in Russia!" I teased as we gave each other a hug.

Then Mrs. Jones knocked on the door and handed Jamie some candy bars and soda pop for the team. As the snack was being passed around Mr. Richards begged for everyone's attention.

"The officials have given me the stats for today's game," he announced. "Listen up if you're interested."

Of course, every guy wanted to know how well he had played, so we all listened closely as Mr. Richards read the statistics.

"Sergi made three passes, two blocks, and four take-aways. Boris had two assists, one of which was for the winning goal. Chevy scored our first goal and had a three-goal hat trick."

"Yea, Chevy!" everyone shouted.

"Thank you! Thank you!" replied Louie as he raised his hands and humbly nodded his head.

"Back to the stats!" ordered Mr. Richards. "Ivan, you had four take-aways, an assist, and our first penalty!"

"Way to go, Ivan!" shouted Louie.

Mr. Richards continued, "Victor had seven blocks, four passes, and a goal. Tretyak, our goalie, had a remarkable game with seventeen saves, and Vladimir had two goals, including the game-winning goal! The rest of you players played a great game and helped your teammates win."

Everyone cheered and whistled, and by this time we were half dressed and quite a sorry sight with sweaty hair and chocolate smudges all over our faces.

"Your parents are waiting," hollered Mr. Fisher. "If you want a ride home, you'd better hustle."

I was exhausted. I finally got my things together and met my family in the lobby.

"Good job, Andy," said Mom as she gave me a hug.

"Yeah," agreed James. "You guys played good for your first game."

"Thanks," I answered.

"Your hair sure is sweaty," added Chrissy. "And you need a shower."

"We'll make him sit in the back," teased Dad.

"Or I could drive," I suggested, "and everyone else can sit in the back."

"You guys will be driving soon enough," said Dad. "I'm happy to be your chauffeur for a few more years."

CHAPTER SEVEN

It was Monday afternoon. I had all I could do to keep my eyes open in health class because it was so boring. At times like this I wondered if maybe going to the Zoo School with Louie wouldn't be such a bad idea. I watched the second hand on the clock jump from one digit to the next. The long, skinny, red hand jerked when it moved around the face of the clock as if it had the hiccups. Only ten more minutes and the buzzer would dismiss us for the day. Every time I heard the buzzer at school, it reminded me of the hockey game. I still couldn't believe that Louie got a hat trick in our first game. I wondered if I'd ever be able to play that well.

"Pass your assignments forward, please," instructed Mr. Reed.

I handed my paper to Jason Potts, who unfortunately was sitting in front of me.

"How do you always get your homework done on time?" asked Jason.

"I just do," I answered, stating the obvious.

"Did you get A's at your other school too?" continued Jason.

"We didn't get letter grades at my other school," I explained. "We got numbers instead."

"Numbers?" inquired Jason. "That's weird!"

"Yeah," I answered, "I thought so too."

By this time Jason was really getting on my nerves, and I was about to tell him to mind his own business when the buzzer sounded and everyone quickly vanished from the classroom. As I was walking toward my locker, I noticed Mr. Fisher in the crowd.

"Hey, Mr. Fisher!" I called out.

"Hi, Ivan," replied Mr. Fisher. "That was quite a game on Saturday!"

"I'm glad we won," I added. "I just hope we can keep it up."

"Your next game is going to be a lot tougher," he said "Those out-of-town kids get more practice than we do. And besides, we're playing on their ice."

"With our goalie, we can handle anything," I answered just as Jimmy walked by.

"Oh, right!" exclaimed Jimmy. "Nothin' like putting all the pressure on me! Pine Creek is tough. Last year my team never beat 'em."

"We'll just have to be tougher," I answered.

"Well, guys," said Mr. Fisher, "I've got papers to grade. Why don't you go home and play a little street hockey?"

"We would," teased Jimmy, "but we have too much homework."

"Yeah," I added, "our English teacher really pours it on."

"You guys are too much!" exclaimed Mr. Fisher, shaking his head as he walked away.

Jimmy and I talked in the hallway for a while until it was time to leave.

"Hey, maybe we can play street hockey together sometime," I suggested, hoping he'd invite me over.

"A bunch of us are playing at Manhatten Park after school tomorrow," he said. "Why don't you come?"

"I'll be there," I answered. "See ya tomorrow."

"Yeah," said Jimmy. "See ya."

When I got home from school, my mom was on the phone talking to Mr. Richards.

"I'm sure we can get him there," she said. "Thanks for calling."

"Get me where?" I asked as soon as she hung up.

"To an off-ice practice at Madison School on Wednesday," she explained. "Mr. Richards said to wear a good pair of tennis shoes and put a sock on the end of your stick so it doesn't scratch the floor."

"With all this hockey practice," I said, "I guess I won't have time for homework."

"With all this hockey practice," said Mom, "I guess you won't have time for television."

•   •   •

On Tuesday after school, I put on my Roller Blades, grabbed my hockey stick, and headed for Manhatten Park.

"Hey, Ivan," said Jimmy as I joined the guys on the pavement.

"Ivan?" questioned Duffy, "I thought your name was Andy."

47

"Ivan's my Dynamo name," I explained.

"Oh, that's right," added Duffy. "I saw the Russian names on your jerseys. Jimmy's name is Tripper."

"It's Tretyak, not Tripper," corrected Jimmy.

"Well, how am I supposed to know?" responded Duffy. "They're weird names, anyway."

"We may have weird names," agreed Jimmy, "but we're the best Squirt team in the league."

"Like heck, you are!" corrected Duffy. "Rocky's Wave Runners are the best."

"Oh, yeah?" argued Jimmy. "What makes you think you know everything?"

"I just do!" answered Duffy.

I was relieved when a few more kids showed up 'cause I was beginning to wonder if Jimmy and Duffy were really going to start fighting.

"Let's play," said Jimmy. "Ivan, you can be on my team."

"Okay," I responded. I didn't even know who the other kids were, but as long as we had enough for two teams, it really didn't matter. We played three-on-three hockey for almost an hour until Duffy said he had to go home.

"I gotta go, too," I said, knowing that my mom was expecting me for dinner and that I had homework to do. "Thanks for letting me play."

"Thanks for comin'," answered Jimmy. "I'll let ya know when we're playin' again."

I really had fun playing street hockey at Manhatten Park, but it wasn't half as much fun as the off-ice practice in Madison School's gymnasium. Playing in tennis shoes on the wooden floor took the advantage away from the faster skaters. Even the rookies could keep up with everyone else.

Running back and forth across the gym floor was exhausting, and it didn't take long before everyone was huffing and puffing.

"Hey, Coach," begged Jamie, "how about a break?"

"All right," agreed Mr. Richards. "We'll take a five minute sissy break."

"Hey, Mr. Richards," I asked, "how did we get to use the gym?"

"The principal's a friend of mine," he answered. "Hey, what's with this Mr. Richards stuff? If you're on the team, you'd better call me Coach Lou. Got it?"

"Got it, Coach," I answered.

"Good," he said. "Sissy break is over. Back on the floor!"

After another round of floor hockey, Coach Lou broke us up into small groups to work on passing.

"Petr and Boris," he announced, "you may work with Ivan and Chevy if you can stay out of trouble."

"Well, at least I won't get hit with a golf ball this time," I remarked.

We worked on passing until we were so tired we could hardly walk.

"Great practice, guys!" praised Coach Lou. "Friday night we'll have practice at the arena, and Saturday's game is at three o'clock in Pine Creek. If your parents can't get you there, call me and I'll see to it that you get a ride. We need all our players for this game."

"I might need a ride," said Billy. "My grandma's in the hospital, so I don't know if my mom and dad can bring me."

"He can ride with me," I offered.

"Great!" said Coach Lou. "Ivan, you're in charge of getting Billy to the game."

"Ivan, you're in charge of not getting any more penalties," teased Jamie.

Everyone burst out laughing.

"Hey, that goes for all of you guys," added Coach Lou. "This team is going to be a challenge. We don't need any power plays working against us!"

With that comment practice was over and the players went home. School went pretty well the next two days, and I even managed to put up with Jason Potts.

CHAPTER EIGHT

On Friday night, we had one of the toughest practices ever. Obviously, the coaches didn't believe in going easy on us before a game.

The next day, we picked up Jimmy and Billy to drive to the game in Pine Creek. About half way there, we stopped for a burger in Jamestown. Jimmy, Billy, and I sat at a table by ourselves. Mom, Dad, and Chrissy — who had to tag along because she had no choice — sat at another table.

"I'm sorry your grandma's sick," I said to Billy.

"She has cancer," replied Billy. "It's spreading pretty fast, and there's not much the doctors can do."

I had no idea Billy's grandma was that sick. I don't like talking about diseases and dying so I changed the subject.

"Do you think we can win today?" I asked.

"We have a chance," answered Jimmy, "but it's only our second game."

"These guys aren't in our league anyway," added Billy, "so even if we lose it won't hurt our record."

"Yeah," I agreed, "even if they beat us we can still be the Squirt champions."

"I'm not so sure about that," said Billy. "I've got

a friend on Rocky's Wave Runners. Their team is supposed to be the best in our league."

"Well, we'll just have to wait and see," I replied. I was getting tired of hearing about how great Rocky's Wave Runners were and was looking forward to playing them. After we finished our burgers, we all piled into the van and finally made it to Pine Creek.

The ice arena at Pine Creek was brand new. It had two full sheets of ice and the fanciest locker room I had ever seen. While we were getting ready for the game, Coach Lou gave us some final instructions.

"Just remember what we worked on in practice," he said. "These guys are big on scoring, so our defense has to be strong."

I swallowed hard. I hoped I could keep the Pine Creek players from scoring too many goals.

"Any questions?" asked Coach Lou.

"Will we get a treat after the game?" asked Jamie. "I didn't eat much breakfast."

Everyone laughed at Jamie's question.

"Well, Boris," answered Coach Lou, "that wasn't the kind of question I had in mind, but, yes, there will be a treat. I think it was Alexi's turn to bring something. Now let's get out on the ice!"

"Let's go Dynamos!" shouted Louie as he led the way.

The Pine Creek players were already warming up. I didn't think they looked so tough. One thing was certain — we sure had better-looking jerseys! Pine Creek's jerseys were orange and black, and the players looked like a bunch of pumpkins.

The Dynamos won the face-off, but everything went downhill from there. The Pine Creek team played so fast we could hardly keep up with them. They scored four unanswered goals in the first period, which made us feel defenseless. I was surprised that Coach Lou stayed so calm.

"You guys are playing well," he said. "Keep up the good work, and let's try to score."

Fortunately, we had a great comeback in the second period. Louie, Benny, and Kurt all managed to score goals, and Jimmy did an outstanding job of keeping the puck out of the net. Then, near the end of the second period, Jamie got mad at one of the Pine Creek players and knocked him down. We were all surprised that he didn't get a penalty. I overheard one of the refs talking to Coach Lou.

"I'll let it go this time," he said, "but if number nine does it again I'm going to give her a penalty!"

As the ref skated away, Coach Lou burst out laughing. "The ref thinks Boris is a girl!" he said. "That's why he didn't give him a penalty! Maybe a few more of you guys should grow your hair long."

In the third period, the Pine Creek pumpkins were just too tough for the Dynamos. They scored two more goals while the Dynamos only scored one. We lost the game with a score of six to four.

Back in the locker room, we listened while Coach Lou went over the statistics.

"I'm sorry we didn't win," said Coach Lou, "but all of you played a good game, and I'm proud of you."

I couldn't believe what I was hearing! I thought for sure we'd get yelled at for losing.

"Tretyak, our goalie, stopped nineteen shots," continued Coach Lou. "Chevy, Sergei, and Vladimir scored one goal apiece. Victor, Petr, Ivan, and Igor all had several blocks and passes. Alexi and Mikael led the team in take-aways, and Boris didn't get a penalty because the ref thought he was a girl."

Everyone howled and hooted as poor Jamie turned beat red.

"Maybe we should change his Russian name to Doris," suggested Mike, which made everyone laugh even harder.

"Hey, Boris," said Coach Lou, "you know we're just havin' fun with you, right?"

"I know," replied Jamie. "What's for snack? I'm starving."

Everyone looked over at Denny Smith. He was the quietest kid on the team, and I don't think I'd ever heard him say more than two words.

"So what'd ya bring, Alexi?" I asked.

Denny held up a big white box. "Doughnuts," he replied.

"Hey, everyone," shouted Jamie. "Let's hear it for Alexi!"

Everyone started whistling and cheering as Denny stood there holding the box of doughnuts.

Someone started chanting, "Speech, speech, speech," until all of the players, except Denny, joined in the chant.

To everyone's surprise, Denny climbed up on the

bench, stood up straight, and in a soft but confident voice responded, *"Whaaaat?"*

With that, all the players cheered and roared until Coach Lou and Mr. Fisher had to quiet us down. Denny passed out the doughnuts while the rest of the team acted like they hadn't eaten in weeks.

"You guys are a bunch of vultures!" exclaimed Coach Lou. "Maybe you should try eating breakfast before you play."

"I did!" replied Mike defensively. "I had two pancakes and a bowl of cereal."

"Where on earth does all your food go?" I asked him. "Your body isn't big enough for all that."

"I'm storing it in my intestines," explained Mike. "Then some day I'm going wake up and be six feet tall."

"Well, you sure play like you're six feet tall," said Coach Lou. "In fact, all of you guys are playing well. We've got a great season ahead of us, and I'm really fired up about our team."

"Hey, Coach," I said. "Wouldn't it be cool if everyone scored a goal this year?"

"That'd be great, Ivan," Coach Lou replied. "But that's a pretty tall order and doesn't usually happen at this level."

"Well, let's make it happen!" I suggested.

"Yeah," replied Louie. "Let's make a pact that we'll all help each other score a goal."

With that suggestion, we all went around giving each other high-fives and chanting, "Score! Score! Score!"

Just then Mr. Jones came into the locker room.

"Your parents are getting restless," he said. "It's a long walk home, so I suggest you guys get movin'."

With that announcement, everyone zipped up their bags and vanished from the locker room.

On the way home, Billy and Jimmy both fell asleep. I was tired, too, but I didn't want to sleep. I just wanted to think about hockey. I decided then that being a Dynamo was pretty great, and that my coach wasn't so bad after all.

CHAPTER NINE

I was actually beginning to like school. Not the home-work, of course, but I liked being at North Middle. Every noon I ate lunch with Jimmy and Duffy, and I didn't feel like a new kid anymore.

This noon, when I was eating my lunch, someone threw a French fry that hit me right in the face.

"What's with this?" I asked as I picked up the fry.

"It's a French fry," answered Duffy, "and it's called a food fight."

Before I knew it, Duffy threw a half-eaten cookie at another kid, and soon food was flying everywhere. I had a carrot I didn't especially want, so I sent it sailing through the air. It landed in a girl's hair. She screamed and cried as though her cat had just died. Ms. Bowens entered the lunchroom at that particular moment, and needless to say, a few of us ended up in the principal's office.

"The food in your lunch bags is intended to be eaten," lectured Mr. Conners, "not thrown at other students. Each of you will be getting a demerit and a note to take home to your parents. I don't want to see you in my office again this year. Is that clear?"

We all nodded our heads in agreement, and I

thought how weird it must be for Duffy to have his dad as the principal.

"Are you going to get it when you get home?" I asked Duffy as we left the office.

"Oh, yeah," answered Duffy. "I'll probably be grounded for a few days. How about you?"

"I don't know," I said. "I've never gotten in trouble at school before."

"Well, good luck," said Duffy as we both headed to our next class.

"Thanks," I said, "I'll need it."

•   •   •

When I got home from school, I told my mom what happened and gave her the note to sign.

"Andy, you know better," she sighed. "You shouldn't have gotten involved. I don't want this to happen again, do you understand?"

"What happened?" asked Chrissy as she walked in the door.

"None of your beeswax," I answered.

"This doesn't concern you," Mom explained. "And please hang up your jacket. I'm tired of finding it on the floor."

"May I go now?" I asked Mom, hoping my lecture was over.

"I want you to do your homework and then get ready for practice," she answered.

I wanted to remind her that it was Friday, and I had the whole weekend to do my homework, but under the circumstances I decided it was in my best interest to do what she said.

That night, when my dad drove Jimmy and me to hockey practice, he didn't say anything about the food fight, so I figured Mom didn't tell him. I was hoping Jimmy wouldn't bring it up.

"Hey, that's a cool song," exclaimed Jimmy, "turn it up."

"Good taste!" responded my dad, as I silently groaned. The last thing I needed was for Jimmy to like my dad's music.

"Shah-na-na-na — shah-na-na-na — hey, hey, hey — good-bye."

Actually, it wasn't a bad tune, but I was glad when we finally got to the rink so I didn't have to listen to it anymore.

As I was getting dressed for practice, a small boy walked in with a huge bag of equipment. I figured he was in the wrong locker room.

"Hey, kid," I said, trying to be helpful, "the Mites are in the other locker room. This is for Squirts only."

"I am a Squirt," he said nervously.

"Who are you?" asked Jamie.

"Freddie Rogers," he replied. "I'm supposed to be on the Dynamos."

The locker room was dead silent. Jamie and I looked at each other in disbelief.

"How old are you?" I asked.

"Ten," replied Freddie.

"Well," I said, "then I guess you're in the right place 'cause we're the Dynamos."

Freddie was about the same size as Mike and was not quite what we had in mind.

"So did you get your tonsils out?" asked Jamie trying to make conversation.

"Yup," Freddie replied.

"Did it hurt?" continued Jamie.

"No," Mike added sarcastically, "it felt so good he wants to have them out again!"

Everyone started laughing, and poor Freddie looked like he was going to cry.

"Hey, guys," I said, "if this kid's a Dynamo, then we better treat him like one."

"Okay," agreed Mike and Jamie. "We'll be nice."

Freddie looked relieved and began getting on his equipment.

"So how long have ya been playin'?" asked Jamie.

"This is my second year," answered Freddie.

As a few of us exchanged glances, I hoped that Freddie didn't notice the doubtful expressions on our faces. Just then Louie and Coach Lou walked into the room.

"Ten minutes and we're on the ice," he announced. "Hey, Freddie, good to see you. If you get tired, let me know. We don't want to work you too hard on your first practice."

"What about us?" asked Jamie. "You work us too hard every week."

"Yeah," added Mike, "you're the toughest coach I've ever had!"

"What a bunch of sissies!" teased Coach Lou. "Stop whining and get your butts out on the ice!"

After skating laps and working on team tactics, Coach Lou told everyone to practice shooting and passing with Mr. Fisher. I was surprised when he called me over to talk to him.

"Ivan," said Coach Lou, "I'm impressed with your positive attitude and hard work. Your skating is improving every week, and you're a smart player. You seem to have a good understanding of the plays and strategies — I can tell you've been studying the playbook — but you need to work harder on your stick handling. I'm going to work with you on it tonight, and I'm also going to give you a bucket of pucks so you can work on it at home."

"Okay, Coach," I answered.

"Keep your stick on the ice and use your wrists more," he instructed.

I listened closely to everything Coach Lou said and tried to follow his advice exactly. I really enjoyed working one-on-one with him. He helped me a lot, and I promised I'd work hard on stick handling at home.

When we finally got off the ice and out of our skates, Coach Lou announced that we were going to do some conditioning exercises. We all moaned and groaned as we put on our tennis shoes and lined up for the exercises.

"I want you to hop on one foot four times, and then on the other foot four times," said Coach Lou. "Keep switching back and forth, and we'll try to do this for three minutes."

I still had the song in my head that we had heard

on the way to practice. As we were hopping up and down, I started singing, "Shah-na-na-na — shah-na-na-na — hey, hey, hey — good-bye." Then everyone else joined in, and we all sang "Sha-na-na-na" as we jumped up and down.

Coach Lou shook his head and smiled. He was pretty impressed when we all lasted the entire three minutes.

"From now on," he said, "Ivan will be in charge of entertaining us while we do our exercises. You guys are all done for tonight. I'll see you tomorrow morning right here at eighty-thirty sharp. We're playing Tony's Pizza. It should be a pretty close game. Remember what we worked on and get a good night's sleep."

•   •   •

The game was close in the first period — zero to zero! In the second period, Tony's Pizza scored three goals, and we remained scoreless. Coach Lou got us together and tried to help.

"You guys aren't playing as a team," he said. "Look for an open player and work on passing. It's not too late to get into the game."

In the third period Louie stole the puck and went for a breakaway. He shot the puck at the net but it hit the post and bounced back. To everyone's amazement, Freddie caught the rebound and scored.

"That's more like it!" shouted Coach Lou. "Do it again!"

We really made an effort to keep the puck in our

offensive zone. Then Mike made a pass to Jamie, who shot and scored.

"Way to go!" shouted Coach Lou. "Now we're in the game."

With a score of three to two, we still had hopes of catching up. Our hopes were soon shattered, however, as Tony's Pizza scored in the last few minutes and won the game four to two.

In the locker room after the game, we were all pretty quiet as Coach Lou was about to read the stats.

"I know you're disappointed that we didn't win," he said, "but listen to the stats. They're not that bad: Trekyak had a remarkable game with twenty-one saves. Victor had eight take-aways and five passes, Sergei had six take-aways and four passes, Chevy had five shots on goal — unfortunately their goalie stopped the puck each time. Ivan, Vladimir, and Mikael all had several take-aways, and Igor had two take-aways, four passes, and a shot on goal. Petr passed to Boris, who scored, and Nikolai had a great goal off a rebound."

"Yea, Nikolai!" shouted Jamie.

"Good game, Nikolai," I added.

"Thanks," answered Freddie.

"Hey, where's the food?" asked Jamie.

"Tony's Pizza is treating us," answered Coach Lou.

"Really?" replied Jamie excitedly.

"Not really," teased Coach Lou.

"That was mean!" exclaimed Jamie.

"I know," Coach Lou said with a laugh. "I never said I was nice."

Ricky passed out granola bars and juice boxes as we got out of our hockey clothes and into our jeans. We now had a record of two losses and one win. If we didn't start winning some games, we'd never have a chance at being the league champions.

CHAPTER TEN

"I have an assignment for you that I think you'll enjoy," announced Mr. Fisher in English class. "I know most of you are interested in rap music. On the surface, rap appears to be quite simplistic, but actually it is rather complex and much more difficult to write than you would think."

He always talked fancy like that when we were in class, but at the hockey rink he talked like one of the guys. And Jimmy was right — I did get used to having Mr. Fisher for a coach as well as my English teacher.

"I would like each of you to write a rap this week," he continued. "I want you to write about something you are especially interested in. I trust you will use good judgment in selecting a topic."

I knew right away what I was going to write about — hockey, of course, and what it was like to be a Dynamo. Mr. Fisher let us work on our raps during class, so I had a pretty good start by the time the bell rang.

I worked on my rap all week long. This was one assignment I didn't mind doing. On Friday, when we had to read ours in front of the class, I volunteered to go first. I wanted to get the reading part over with as soon as possible.

Yo, we're the Dynamos and we're here to say,
When we come to the rink, we come to play!
We hit and check 'cause we're all nuts,
And we guarantee we'll kick your butts!

Our jerseys are yellow, our jerseys are black,
We'll hit you so hard you'll be layin' on your back!
Our coach is cool, his name is Lou,
He'll tell ya how to play, he'll tell ya what to do.

Our team is awesome, our team is rad,
Hey, we're so good we'll make ya look bad!
We're a Russian team, we're big and mean,
And we will surely make you scream!

Word to your goalie — the Dynamos are comin'!

I was surprised when everyone clapped.

"Excellent rap, Ivan," said Mr. Fisher.

"Ivan?" asked Jason Potts.

"That's right," explained Mr. Fisher. "At school he's Andy, but at hockey he's Ivan. And since this rap is about hockey, I think it would be appropriate for his pen name to be Ivan."

From that day on, almost everyone in the whole middle school knew I played hockey and that Mr. Fisher was one of my coaches.

I listened as everyone else read their raps. Some

were boring and some were pretty funny. Then there was Jason Potts, who wrote about the time he found an earthworm in his grilled cheese sandwich. I was glad when class was finally over.

"Hey, Ivan!" called Mr. Fisher as I was almost out of the room. "If you bring your rap to practice tonight, I'll give you an A+ instead of an A. I want Coach Lou to see it."

"Sure," I answered. "I'll do anything for an A+."

"Good," he replied. "I'll see you tonight."

·　·　·

After hockey practice that evening, Mr. Fisher announced that I had something to share with the team. He made me stand up on the bench and read my rap to Coach Lou and all of the players.

Yo, we're the Dynamos and we're here to say,
When we come to the rink, we come to play.
We hit and check 'cause we're all nuts,
And we guarantee we'll kick your butts.

As I continued reading the rap, the kids started clapping their hands and tapping their feet. Then, when Jamie stood up on the bench and started dancing, everyone else got up and danced. I finished reading the rap, and the players all cheered and whistled.

"Fantastic rap, Ivan!" exclaimed Coach Lou. "I want you to make copies for everyone. From now on, this will be our official team rap. We'll recite it after every practice and before every game. I want all of you to memorize it this week."

Everyone started talking and laughing until Coach Lou whistled and quieted things down.

"About tomorrow's game," he said, "we've got a good chance against these guys. They're two for one, and their goalie is a rookie. It's a morning game, so go home and go to bed. I'll see you bright and early at seven."

"You guys seem pretty fired up," my dad said on the way home.

"That's because we're gonna win tomorrow," I answered.

"Is that right?" asked Dad.

"That's right!" agreed Jimmy. "And it's time we start putting fear into our opponents."

"Who do you play tomorrow?" Dad asked.

"De Young's Furniture," I answered. "We're going to crush them to pieces."

"That's Coach Johnson's team, Andy," Dad reminded me, "the team you were supposed to be on before you were traded."

"Well," I answered, "maybe after tomorrow Coach Johnson will be sorry I got traded."

My dad shook his head. "I don't know what happened at practice tonight," he said, "but you guys seem pretty confident."

"It's the rap," replied Jimmy.

"What rap?" Dad asked.

"Oh, it's just the rap I wrote for English," I explained. "I'll read it to you when we get home."

"I can hardly wait," replied Dad.

Seven in the morning was much too early as far as I was concerned! I was barely awake, and here I was sitting in the locker room with the rest of the Dynamos listening to Coach Lou's instructions.

"I know it's early," said Coach Lou, "but you'll feel better when you get on the ice. The cold air will wake you up."

"We should have stayed here over night," said Jamie.

"Then you wouldn't have gotten any sleep!" exclaimed Coach Lou. "At least by going home you got a few hours. At any rate, I've decided to make a few changes, so listen closely. I think that Nikolai proved he's a tough hockey player — even without his tonsils! I'm putting him on defense with Petr. Because they're both small, our opponents won't pay much attention to them. They'll be one of our secret weapons, and we'll call them our micro defense."

Everyone smiled and listened as Coach Lou continued.

"I want Ivan and Igor to play wing today. Let's see what you guys can do at the net. The rest of you will be playing your regular positions. It's time to go out on the ice, so I want Ivan to lead us in the rap."

I began reciting the rap. All of the players joined in. I couldn't believe how fast they had learned it — especially since I hadn't even passed out the copies!

When I finished the rap I shouted, "Who's gonna win?"

"We are!" shouted the Dynamos.

"Who's gonna lose?"

"They are!"

"What do we do when we get the puck?"

"Score!"

"What?"

"Score!"

From that day on, I was the official "cheerleader" before every game.

The players for De Young's Furniture were tough, but Jimmy's goal-tending was tougher. No matter how hard they tried, they just couldn't score. Louie scored two goals in the first period, and Kurt scored a goal in the second. In the third period, Benny passed to me right in front of the net. I couldn't believe it when I shot the puck into the net! My first goal of the season! I decided I liked playing wing as much as defense.

Talk about defense — the micro defense turned out to be a good strategy. Freddie and Mike did a great job of keeping the puck in our offensive zone and helping Jimmy at the net. Ricky Clay was having a great game, too. He was so aggressive that he had more take-aways by himself than half the team put together. We won the game four to zero. That was more like it! A few more games like this and we'd be champions for sure!

"I'm sorry I let you go, Andy," said Coach Johnson as we passed each other in the lineup. "Good game."

"Good game," I answered as I shook his hand.

One thing was certain, I was glad I was wearing a Dynamo jersey rather than a furniture store jersey!

"Everyone had a great game," said Coach Lou in the locker room, "but here are a few highlights: Tretyak had his first shutout of the season, and Ivan scored his first goal. Petr and Nikolai were strong on micro defense, and Chevy scored the first two goals of the game. Igor proved today that he is definitely a morning person! Igor had an unbelievable game with nineteen take-aways!"

"He played like a lion after its prey," remarked Mr. Fisher.

"Yeah," added Louie, "I think he was after some raw meat."

Ricky smiled at all the attention, and from then on everyone called him "Raw Meat Igor."

It was Billy's turn to provide the snack that day. While he was passing out bagels and orange juice, Coach Lou continued talking to the players.

"I'm really proud of every player on this team," he said. "I'm impressed with how well you're playing together and how you're using the plays and strategies that we work on in practice. But what impresses me the most is how well all of you get along. We're having as much fun in the locker room as we are on the ice — which is why we have such great team spirit. I just want you to know that I'm proud to be your coach and that in all my years of coaching, I've never had a team like this."

The locker room was really quiet because the players didn't quite know how to respond. We weren't used to Coach Lou being so serious. Just then, Jamie let out a rip-roaring belch. The whole team went into hysterics.

Coach Lou shook his head. "How am I going to survive the rest of this year!" he exclaimed. "You guys are impossible. Now get out of here and go home. I'll see you Friday night."

CHAPTER ELEVEN

The Dynamos were on a roll. We won the next six games, and Jimmy had five shutouts in a row. Everyone in the league was talking about Jimmy's shutouts, and no one could remember any other goalie having five in a row. Coach Lou knew some woman that worked at a TV station who said she wanted to put us on the news.

When Jimmy's mom dropped us off for practice, the television crew was already there. Mrs. Cleaver was so excited that she decided to stay and watch. Coach Lou gave us a few pointers as we were getting dressed.

"Remember to be polite, guys," instructed Coach Lou, "and just act normal. They want to film us while we practice, and then they're going to interview Jimmy and ask us some questions."

While Coach Lou was talking, Jamie and Mike began making silly faces and acting like weirdos.

"You guys are hopeless!" exclaimed Coach Lou. "I give up."

The television people were waiting for us when we came out on the ice. Some guy with a huge camera started filming us as we skated around the rink. It was hard to act normal and pretend they weren't there.

"Look at Mike," whispered Louie.

"Hi, Mom!" hollered Mike as he skated right in front of the camera waving. It didn't take Jamie long to get into the act either. Soon everyone was waving and trying to get on camera.

"I'm sorry," Coach Lou said to the camera guy as he gave us a dirty look.

"No problem," he answered. "I got some good shots."

"That's what I'm afraid of!" replied Coach Lou.

"Let's have a chat with the goalie," said the camera man.

"He's over there," said Louie pointing toward Jimmy.

The camera man filmed Jimmy while some woman asked him a bunch of questions.

"How long have you been playing goalie?" she asked.

"This is my second year," replied Jimmy.

"I hear you've had five shutouts in the last six games," she continued.

Jimmy nodded his head. "That's right," he said.

"What makes you so good?" asked the woman.

"Lot's of practice," Jimmy replied.

"Well, I hope you continue to do well," she said as she faced the camera. "That's the story from Grand City Ice Arena. Back to you, Charles."

As the guy turned off his camera, everyone started clapping and whistling, and I wondered who in the world Charles was.

"You'll be on tomorrow at six," the woman told

us as she quickly gathered up her things and disappeared with the camera man.

"All right, guys," shouted Coach Lou, "back to practice!"

It was almost impossible to concentrate on our drills. We all kept talking about the interview and wondered if we'd see ourselves on TV.

"If you guys don't get serious," threatened Coach Lou, "we'll do an hour of conditioning exercises."

With that announcement, we got our minds back on hockey practice and started paying attention. We did a few more drills, then we practiced shooting for the rest of the time.

I was glad I had finally scored a few goals. Louie was leading the team with sixteen goals, and Kurt was in second place with eight. Benny had scored four goals, Raw Meat Igor and I had three, Jamie and Mark had two, and Mike and Freddie each had one goal apiece. Billy and Denny hadn't scored a goal yet, but I knew it was just a matter of time. After all, we had made a pact that everyone would score, and the Dynamos would be true to their word.

I was glad when practice was finally over. In the locker room, Coach Lou gave us some tips for tomorrow's game.

"Tomorrow we're playing a team from Oakwood's league," he said. "You know they have a bad attitude toward any team in our league and they like to play dirty. Their record is only five and four, but last week they beat Rocky's Wave Runners, who happen to be in first place in our league."

"We can beat 'em!" said Louie confidently.

"Yeah," said Jamie, "we'll spill their guts all over the ice."

"I know how we can beat them," said Mike with a smile that was almost as big as his face.

"How's that?" asked Coach Lou.

"Score more goals than they do," he replied.

"Well," remarked Coach Lou, "that's the best strategy I've heard in a long time. I think it might work!"

As we were leaving the locker room Coach Lou called out, "Remember, guys — no women, no booze, and be in bed by ten!"

• • •

I couldn't believe how big the Oakwood players were! We looked like midgets compared to them. I had heard rumors that some of the Oakwood players lied about their ages. Judging by some of their sizes, I figured the rumors were probably true.

"Size is not important," reminded Coach Lou as we were preparing to send out our first line. "We need to be quick and outskate them. Don't be intimidated by their size."

"I won't be," said Mike, "if they stay away from me!"

The buzzer sounded and the players took their positions on the ice. Raw Meat Igor and I were playing wing and the micro defense was as ready as ever. Louie was playing center and won the face-off for the Dynamos. He passed the puck to Raw Meat, who skated it toward the net and took a shot. The puck hit the post and bounced right in front of the net where I happened to be. I slapped the puck past the goalie and into the net. The Dynamos went wild as I scored the first goal of the game.

It seemed as though my goal started something that couldn't be stopped. Louie scored two more goals in the first period, and Kurt and Benny both scored in the second. Oakwood finally scored a goal, but it didn't look like they would ever catch up.

In the third period, things got ugly. Oakwood started playing dirty and went after Louie. One of their players knocked Louie down, slashing him in the arm with a stick.

"Help Louie off the ice!" shouted Coach Lou.

Louie was hurting badly.

"Hey, ref," yelled Coach Lou, "you can open your eyes now!"

Coach Lou was furious. Louie had to sit out for the rest of the game, and Oakwood didn't even get a penalty. I couldn't remember a time when Coach Lou was that angry. Mr. Fisher stepped in to coach and told Coach Lou to cool down.

The Oakwood team scored another goal with three minutes left in the game. We were leading five to two, and were pretty optimistic about the game, until another Oakwood player went after little Mike Hanson, punching him right in the gut and knocking him down. I was so angry I went out on the ice and started hitting the bully. Jamie and Kurt quickly joined in, and so did some of the Oakwood players. Soon sticks and gloves were flying everywhere.

"Break it up!" screamed a referee as he tried to pull us apart.

"You're out of the game!" yelled the other referee, though I wasn't quite sure who he was yelling at.

Kurt, Jamie, and I got sent to the penalty box for the rest of the game with ten-minute major penalties. Good thing there were only two minutes left in the game! The bully from Oakwood was thrown out of the game and given a game misconduct. The parents and fans were yelling and screaming so loudly that the referees wouldn't continue the game until everyone calmed down.

With Louie and Mike injured, and the three of us serving penalties, there wasn't much left of the Dynamo team. Benny, Mark, and Raw Meat Igor went out on the ice for the first remaining minute, while Denny, Freddie, and Billy finished up the last minute of the game.

"Thank goodness!" shouted Jamie as the last few seconds ticked away and the buzzer ended the game.

We decided to get the handshake over with as quickly as possible to avoid another brawl.

"Pighead!" muttered an Oakwood player as we started going through the line.

"Sissy face!" said another.

Some of them even spit in their hands before shaking.

"Don't say anything," advised Louie, as we finished the lineup. "Go to the locker room."

"That was quite a game," remarked Coach Lou as we gathered in the locker room. "I knew these guys were rough, but I never expected what happened today. I'm proud of the way you played and the way you defended yourselves. I'm just thankful that no one else got hurt. I'm planning on writing a letter to the hockey association, and maybe this team will get put on probation. Anyway, we won the game and hung tough 'til the end. I'm especially proud of the players who survived the game and finished the last few minutes for our team. I'm going to ask Mr. Fisher to read the stats while I get some more ice for Louie's arm and make sure Mike is okay."

Louie's eyes got all red and watery. Mike was sitting on the bench next to Louie, holding his stomach.

"I hope we never have to play those jerks again," I said loud enough for everyone to hear.

"Fortunately," said Mr. Fisher, "they're only on our schedule one time. Now, here are today's stats."

In his best teacher's voice, Mr. Fisher read the stats, but no one seemed interested. Winning wasn't much fun when the game turned out like this one did. I don't really know what made me do it, but for some reason I stood up and started reciting the rap.

Yo, we're the Dynamos and we're hear to say,
When we come to the rink, we come to play!
We hit and check 'cause we're all nuts,
But we guarantee we'll kick your butts!

One by one the players joined in, and soon everyone was smiling and dancing around the locker room. When we finished the rap, Coach Lou came over and gave me a hug.

"Thanks, Ivan. We needed that. Hey, by the way, guys," he continued, "next week is Thanksgiving. The team from London is coming, and we'll be playing them Friday afternoon since you don't have school."

"All right!" shouted Jamie as everyone cheered and gave each other high-fives.

"My mom and I were in London this summer," Freddie Rogers spoke up proudly.

"Uh, Freddie," interrupted Louie, "these guys are from London, Ontario — not London, England."

"Yeah," added Jamie, "and they're just as good as the Russians!"

"But we're better than the Russians!" I shouted.

"Yeah," added Mike, who apparently was feeling better. "We'll make 'em wish they stayed home."

"Well, one thing is certain," remarked Coach Lou, "after today, you guys can handle anything!"

CHAPTER TWELVE

On Thanksgiving morning, my family and I went to Mayflower Church, which was right around the corner from where we lived. Mayflower was not the church we usually went to on Sundays, but my mom wanted to go because there was going to be a real Pilgrim service. When we drove into the parking lot, there were two men dressed as Pilgrims playing drums. I had never seen anything like that before!

"Hey, Andy," someone said as I was hanging up my jacket. I looked up and couldn't believe it — Jason Potts!

"Hi, Jason," I answered. Fortunately, I didn't have time to talk to him 'cause my parents were already on their way down the aisle. As I looked around the sanctuary I noticed a few more kids from North Middle, and wondered if they thought we only went to church on Thanksgiving Day.

The service was sort of interesting. For the offering, the deacons passed around bags on long sticks. When the bag passed, you were supposed to put your money in. Chrissy accidentally dropped a piece of candy in the bag along with her dollar bill. Then the deacon gave her a dirty look as she tried to retrieve her candy.

After church, we changed our clothes and joined my aunt, uncle, and cousins at my grandparents' house for dinner. My grandma always cooks enough food to feed the whole neighborhood — she's a great cook!

"Who wants to beat me at pool?" I challenged when we were through eating.

"I'm watching the football game," announced Dad.

"I'm washin' dishes," Grandma said with a laugh.

"And I'm playin' with my cousins," added Chrissy who loved playing with her three little girl cousins.

"I'll take you on," said James. "Football is for couch potatoes."

After five games of pool, a couple hours of watching football, and some enjoyable moments teasing Chrissy, I was more than ready to go home.

"Are you coming to my hockey game tomorrow?" I asked Grandpa and Grandma as we were leaving.

"We're comin'," answered Grandma, "but I don't wanna see any fightin'."

•   •   •

On Friday afternoon, Mom and Dad drove me to the ice rink for our first game against the London team. We were going to play one game on Friday and another on Saturday.

"I hope Louie and Mike are back on top after last week's game," Dad remarked as we walked into the arena.

"They're two of the toughest kids on the team," I answered. "They'll be back."

"Well, I hope this game isn't so rough," Mom replied. "I don't like it when kids get hurt."

"That's part of playing hockey, Mom," I explained. "Ya better get used to it."

"Don't tell that to Grandma," said Mom.

When I went into the locker room I noticed a sign posted on the wall. The sign said: PAIN IS TEMPORARY — PRIDE IS FOREVER!

"Great banner!" I exclaimed. "Who put it up?"

"I did," answered Coach Lou. "I came across this quote yesterday, and after last week's game against Oakwood I thought it was appropriate for our team."

"Pain is temporary," said Mike, "but it sure hurts!"

Everyone laughed at Mike's remark and began getting dressed for the game.

"The teams from London are first-class teams," remarked Coach Lou. "They play clean and are good sports. I'm anticipating a great game. As a token of our appreciation we're going to give every London player a USA Hockey pin at the beginning of the game. Mr. Fisher is going to pass them out, so make sure you all get one."

Everyone carefully examined the pins as Mr. Fisher handed them out.

"Wow," said Jamie, "these are cool! Can I have one?"

"Sorry, Jamie," answered Mr. Fisher, "we only

have enough for the London players. Ask your parents to get you one for Christmas."

"His list is too long already," piped up Mr. Jones who happened to be in the locker room. "He wants new skates, new pads, a new helmet, and a new pair of roller blades. He thinks money grows on trees."

"It does!" replied Mike, "it grows on Christmas trees!"

"I need a new hockey bag," commented Louie. "I hope I get one for Christmas."

"Me, too," said Jimmy. "And I could use a new pair of gloves."

"Excuse me," interrupted Coach Lou. "I hate to interrupt our social hour here, but we have a game to play. Ivan, lead us in the rap as we move onto the ice."

Yo! We're the Dynamos and we're hear to say,
When we come to the rink, we come to play.

The London team stared at us as we finished the rap in the center of the ice rink:

Word to your goalie — the Dynamos are comin'!

Next, we presented our gifts to the London players.

"Cool pin," said one of the players.

"Wear it proudly," Louie answered seriously, but the rest of us started laughing.

Then both teams formed a line and stood in somber silence as they played the national anthem, which was only done when we hosted a team from

Canada. Actually, I got a little choked up and started thinking about how cool it would be to play the national anthem at every game.

The buzzer sounded, and the puck was in play. Louie intercepted the puck on a pass between two London players. He skated full speed ahead on a breakaway and scored a picture-perfect goal in the opening minutes of the game.

"Yes!" screamed Jamie at the top of his lungs.

"Good job, Louie!" I shouted as he skated toward the bench.

"Great goal, Chevy," said Coach Lou. "But remember, guys, the game has just started and anything can happen."

I really liked playing the London team. They were good skaters and played within the rules. We went the entire first period with no penalties — and no injuries! Kurt scored a goal for the Dynamos in the second period, and London managed to get one by Jimmy as well. We were up two to one at the beginning of the third period.

"You're playing well," said Coach Lou. "But why don't we crank it up a few notches and show them what we can really do."

Raw Meat and I went out to play wing. Benny was at center, and Billy and Denny were playing defense. We passed and skated the puck across the ice into London territory. I passed the puck to Benny, who was in front of the net. He shot the puck — it hit the goalie's skate and bounced back. I have no idea what Billy was doing by the net, since he was supposed to be playing defense, but he happened to be in the right place at the right time. He shot the puck right through the goalie's legs and scored.

"All right, Billy!" I yelled as I gave him a hockey player's hug.

Everyone was happy for Billy, and he was smiling like crazy. But the London team didn't give up. They came back and scored, making it three to two.

"It's still anybody's game," reminded Coach Lou. "Another goal would help, and by all means, don't let them score!"

Louie came through for the team as usual and scored another goal with two minutes left in the game. We managed to keep the London team from scoring, and won the game four to two. We mobbed each other on the ice and acted as if we had just won the Stanley Cup.

In the locker room, Coach Lou had a hard time getting our attention.

"Hey, Mark," he yelled in an attempt to be heard above the noise, "go ahead and pass out the snack. Maybe these maniacs will quiet down if they have food in their mouths."

Mark did as he was told, and Coach Lou was right. Things were much quieter when our mouths were full.

"We all had a great game," announced Coach Lou. "That was the best display of teamwork I've ever seen. You guys are awesome!"

"Hooray for Billy!" shouted Mike.

"Way to go Billy!" everyone yelled.

"Congratulations, Mikail," said Coach Lou as he presented Billy with the puck from the game.

"Thanks," he said beaming from ear to ear.

It was then that I noticed Louie sitting on the bench by himself.

"Hey, what's up?" I asked him.

First he just shrugged his shoulders, then he said, "I'm really happy for Billy and all, but it's just that I score goals every game and no one says anything. Sometimes I get hat tricks and everything, but it doesn't seem like a big deal to anybody."

I really felt sorry for Louie and tried to think of something to say.

"It's just that you're so good, everyone expects you to score," I explained. "And besides, your dad probably doesn't want to make a big deal out of your goals 'cause you're his kid, and he wants to be careful not to brag too much."

"Hey, maybe you're right," Louie said. "I never thought of it that way. I just thought maybe the other guys were jealous or something."

"No one's jealous of you, Louie," I assured him. "We admire you. You're so awesome!"

"Thanks, Ivan," he said. "I'm glad you're on our team."

"Me, too," I answered.

Coach Lou must have read the stats while Louie and I were talking 'cause all of a sudden everyone started leaving.

"The game's at ten tomorrow," reminded Coach

Lou. "Be here by nine, and stay out of jail. We need you!"

•   •   •

It seemed like only a few short hours before I was back in the locker room with the rest of the Dynamos. We were ready for our second game against London.

"Hey," said Jamie, "maybe today they'll give us a gift."

"Yeah," said Mike, "maybe they'll give us a maple leaf pin!"

"Uh, I don't think so," answered Louie. "They only give us a gift when we play them in London."

"So why didn't we get to go there?" asked Mike.

"The teams take turns," explained Louie. "We'll go next year when we're Pee Wees."

"Get your skates laced," instructed Coach Lou. "Five minutes and we're out the door."

"Any words of wisdom, Coach?" I asked.

"Let's just have a repeat performance of yesterday's game," he answered.

"I'll agree to that," added Billy, who was still feeling proud of his goal.

As we stood in line and listened to the national anthem, I noticed that the London team was using a different goalie. Not only that, they were all smiling and looking extra confident. I couldn't wait 'til the nation anthem was over.

"Hey Coach," I whispered. "They got a new goalie."

"You're right, Ivan," he replied. "I didn't notice that."

Without saying anything else, Coach Lou went over to talk to the ref. Then he came back and took me aside.

"This is their regular goalie," he explained. "He got carsick on the way over here yesterday and couldn't play. Don't tell the other guys. It's probably better if they don't know."

I nodded my head in agreement and thought it was kind of neat that Coach Lou and I were the only ones who knew.

The first period was pretty rough. We couldn't get anything past their goalie. Lucky for us, they didn't score either. Louie finally made a goal in the second period — then one of the London players got one, too. At the end of the second period, we were tied one to one.

"What's the deal?" asked Jimmy during our break.

"The deal is, we can't score!" explained Jamie sarcastically.

"They have a different goalie," announced Louie who had finally figured it out.

"Before you guys panic," replied Coach Lou, "let me remind you that we did score one goal. If we scored one, we can score more. Now get out there and score!"

I played on Louie's line in the third period. I liked being on his line, but sometimes it was hard to keep up with him. London had several shots on goal, but Jimmy was too quick to let anything get through. Louie got control of the puck and was skating it toward the net. I skated hard to keep up with him. Then, instead of shooting the puck, he passed it to me in front of the net. I was really surprised, but I hit the puck with all my might and shot it past the goalie and into the net.

"*Yes*, Ivan!" shouted Louie.

Everyone mobbed me on the ice and acted as though I had won the game. It would have been a dream come true, except that London scored near the end of the third period and tied the game.

"You played a great game," praised Coach Lou in the locker room. "We almost won, but a tie is better than a loss. Besides, we're the only Squirt team in our league that has beaten one of the London teams."

With that announcement, the Dynamos started cheering and pouring juice boxes on each others' heads. I couldn't believe how close I came to scoring the winning goal. It could have been the game of my life. I could have been the hero. But then I reminded myself that if Louie hadn't passed me the puck, it wouldn't have been my goal anyway.

CHAPTER THIRTEEN

The weeks between Thanksgiving and Christmas always seem like the longest ones of the year. I still get pretty excited about Christmas, and this year it seemed like Christmas would never come.

My homeroom at school was collecting money and clothing to help out some of the families in our community. I donated some of my favorite sweatshirts that were too small, along with some money I earned doing chores around the house.

I was glad when the weekend finally arrived. Going to practice made the days pass more quickly. On Saturday we had a game in Big Rapids at the state college. We were playing the District 6 Squirt Champs from Big Rapids, and I knew it'd be a miracle if we won. I still couldn't wait to go, because the college had a brand new ice arena, and I knew it'd be fun to play at a big college. Friday night practice turned out to be a typical Friday night practice, except Billy never showed up and no one knew where he was.

"I'll call Billy's mom tonight," said Coach Lou, "and find out why he wasn't here. I hope he's planning on going to Big Rapids tomorrow because we need everyone. This will probably be our toughest game so far, but you guys have improved so much since our first game, I really think we have a chance."

"A chance to get killed!" replied Kurt.

"Yeah," added Jamie, "we're going to get our butts kicked!"

"Come on, guys," encouraged Coach Lou, "that's not the kind of attitude we need for this game. I read a great quote this week that I want you to remember. It goes like this: 'Those who believe they can win have already begun to conquer.'"

"And those who don't go to bed on time," added Mike, "will fall asleep on the way to the game."

"I like Mike's quote better," said Jamie as everyone burst out laughing.

"You guys are the sorriest bunch I've ever seen!" teased Coach Lou. "Now get out of here and go home!"

The early morning drive to Big Rapids was sort of peaceful. Outside the sky was a clear blue and the snow sparkled. I could feel the sun through the window of the van on the arm of my jacket. I was one of the first players to arrive at the college, but one by one the Dynamos rolled in. We found our way to the locker room, which was so new it still smelled of freshly painted walls.

"This really doesn't look like a hockey locker room," I commented. "It's too clean!"

"What this locker room needs is some names scratched on the walls and a few wads of gum stuck to the floor," said Jamie.

"Yeah," agreed Mike, "and I just happen to have a marker in my hockey bag."

"And I've got some gum I'd like to get rid of," added Jimmy.

"I saw a can of spray paint in the bathroom," said Louie.

"I don't think so, boys!" interrupted Mr. Fisher with a horrified look on his face. "Any damage to this locker room will damage our reputation."

"Hey," I said, "we're just kiddin'!"

"With you guys I never know!" Mr. Fisher replied.

When all of the players except Billy were in the locker room, Coach Lou said he needed to talk to us. We knew it was something bad by the look on his face.

"Billy wasn't at practice last night," explained Coach Lou, "because his grandmother died this week. He really wanted to play today, but the funeral is this morning and he can't get here on time. He said to tell you guys to get out there and kick butt!"

Nobody said a word or even moved. For the first time since the beginning of the season there was silence in the locker room. I stared at the floor because I didn't want to look at anyone.

"I know we all feel bad for Billy," said Coach Lou, "but he's gonna be okay, and we've got a game to play. Billy wants us to get out there and play our best."

The players continued to sit motionless on the benches, and I was surprised when Coach Lou asked to see me outside the locker room.

"Ivan," said Coach Lou as we stood in the hall-way, "you may not be wearing a *K* on your jersey, but as far as I'm concerned, you're one of the real leaders of this team. The players all like you, and you have the ability to motivate them."

I listened closely as Coach Lou continued, "Nobody in that room wants to play hockey right now. I don't think there is anything I can do or say to make them want to play. Ivan, I'm asking you to do two things. First of all, I want you to go back in there and fire up the players, and secondly, I want you to play center. Do you think you can you do that?"

"Sure, Coach," I answered trying to sound confident. "I'll do whatever it takes."

I walked back into the locker room with my heart pounding. I wasn't sure what I was going to say, but somehow the words just started coming out of my mouth.

"We didn't come all the way up here to sit around in this locker room," I said. "We've got to get out there and play the toughest game we've ever played as a team. I want to tell Billy that we won our game today, and we're the only ones who can make that happen. Who are we?"

"The Dynamos!" shouted Louie as he stood up.

"Who?"

"The Dynamos!" shouted the rest of the players as they all stood up.

"Who's gonna win?" I asked.

"We are!"

"Who are we?"

"The Dynamos!"

Yo, we're the Dynamos and we're hear to say,
when we come to the rink, we come to play . . .

There was something about reciting the rap that always inspired the team. We went out to the ice really fired up. The fans whistled and cheered when we made our appearance. We wondered where all the people had come from.

When the game was about to begin, I skated to the face-off circle for the first time in my life. I knew I'd remember this moment forever. The referee dropped the puck — I quickly drew up and passed to Benny. Benny skated with the puck and passed to Louie, who tried for a breakaway. We lost the puck to a Big Rapids player who caught up with Louie. The Big Rapids players were aggressive and quickly scored a goal in the first few minutes of the game. We tried our hardest to come back with everything we had, but it wasn't enough. They scored two more goals and were leading three to zero at the end of the first period.

"Don't get discouraged," instructed Coach Lou. "Let's just keep working hard and try to score."

At the beginning of the second period, I took my position in the face-off circle and managed to pass the puck to Raw Meat, who skated it across the line and into our offensive zone. He passed to Louie, who made a second attempt at a breakaway play. This time, however, Louie was successful, and we all went ballistic with our first goal of the game.

Big Rapids started playing faster and harder but it didn't help them score. Jimmy's reflexes were as quick as lightning, and he blocked their repeated shots on goal. With an assist from Benny, Louie managed another goal. Then everyone was in shock when Freddie passed the puck to Mike, who went into the net and scored! At the end of the second period, the game was tied three to three.

"I feel like I'm going to explode!" exclaimed Jamie.

"Me, too," agreed Louie.

"I know you guys are excited," said Coach Lou, "but you need to calm down and keep your heads in the game. You've had a great comeback, but we still have one whole period ahead of us."

The third period was unbelievable! Our team played better than we had ever played before. We somehow managed to keep control of the puck and spent most of the time in our offensive zone.

"Pass to Louie," I shouted to Raw Meat who at that moment was skating with the puck.

Raw Meat must have heard me 'cause he passed the puck to Louie, who rushed in and scored. The District 6 Champs were now down by one and looked as though they had seen a ghost. The fans were going nuts, and no one could believe what was happening. With five minutes left in the game, Louie scored another goal, putting us up by two.

"I smell a victory," exclaimed Jamie as we switched lines.

"They can still catch up," shouted Coach Lou from the bench. "Don't let them score!"

The words were no sooner out of his mouth when

Big Rapids scored another goal. Now they were only trailing by one. With three minutes left in the game, Big Rapids was in control.

"Oh, no!" I shouted as I watched a Big Rapids player skate toward the net with the puck. I felt helpless sitting on the bench. It was all I could do to keep from going out on the ice. A powerful slap shot sent the puck sailing through the air directly toward the net. It could have been the goal that tied the game, but Jimmy saved the day by catching the puck in midair.

"Go ahead, Ivan," Coach Lou said with a nod. "You deserve the last two minutes."

I jumped over the wall and skated as fast as I could to the face-off circle. With everyone in position, the ref dropped the puck and the seconds ticked away. My heart was beating so fast I thought I was going to pass out! I wanted to look at the clock, but I didn't dare take my eyes off the puck. I slapped it to Jamie and he passed it to Mark, who skated it toward the net. With Louie in perfect shooting position, Mark passed the puck to Louie, who shot and scored.

"Oh, yes!" I screamed at the top of my lungs as I joined my teammates mobbing Louie in front of the net.

"It's not over," yelled one of the refs as the other ref blew his whistle in our ears.

Coach Lou had to come out on the ice to help break us up.

"You guys need to finish the game!" he yelled as he tried to pry us apart.

"Come on guys," I chimed in knowing we had to play out the remaining thirty seconds.

We picked up our gloves and sticks and went back to our positions. Big Rapids tried to score, but time ran out and the buzzer seemed like the most wonderful sound I had ever heard in my whole life. We barely had enough strength left to skate through the line and shake hands with the Big Rapids team. They didn't say much, but at least they didn't spit in their hands or call us names. When I walked into the locker room, Coach Lou came up to me and gave me a hug.

"Thanks, Ivan," he said. "I knew you could get this team pumped up, but I never expected what happened today. Our team wouldn't be the same without you."

I got a lump in my throat and could hardly swallow. My eyes started to burn as tears swelled up in my eyes. I knew if I tried to talk I would cry, so I just nodded my head and smiled.

"Let's hear the stats!" shouted Jimmy.

"Yeah," replied Kurt, "we want to know how we did."

"You were awesome!" answered Coach Lou. "And I especially want to thank Ivan for his pep talk and for making us get our butts out there and give it all we had!"

"Three cheers for Ivan!" yelled Louie.

"Hip, hip, hooray!" shouted the Dynamos. "Hip, hip, hooray! Hip, hip, hooray!"

Everyone finally quieted down long enough for Coach Lou to read the stats.

"I am very proud today," said Coach Lou, "not only as a coach, but also as a father. Vyacheslav, better known as Chevy, Louie, or 'The Scoring Machine,' had five goals today — which is a first for his hockey career."

"Yea, Louie!" shouted Jamie.

"Way to go, Louie!" added Kurt.

"I feel a song coming on," I said as everyone looked at me. I stood up on the bench and began singing one of my dad's favorite oldies. "Louie, Lou I, oh, Louie — he scored a goal! Na, na, na, na, na, na. Louie Lou I, oh, baby! He scored five goals."

Everyone joined in singing, even Coach Lou and Mr. Fisher. I looked over at Louie, who was turning purple, and I didn't know if it was from embarrassment or from laughing so hard.

Just then, Mr. Jones came into the locker room. "I have a surprise for you guys," he announced. "We're all going to Casey's for lunch. Denny's dad taped the game, and we can watch it on a big-screen TV while we eat. So hurry up and let's get out of here!"

"Forget the stats," said Coach Lou. "Let's go to Casey's!"

We quickly gathered our things, met our parents, and headed for Casey's, which was only two blocks away. The manager at Casey's let us sit in their banquet room and said he would start the tape as soon as everyone ordered. I looked up from my menu for a second and couldn't believe it when I saw Billy and his mom walk into the room. Billy was all dressed up in a suit and tie and had just come from the funeral.

"Hey, Billy," I asked, "how'd you know we'd be here?"

"Coach Lou told my mom you'd probably eat here after the game," he explained.

"Well, have a seat," I offered as I pulled out a chair next to me.

Billy sat down and tried to get in on the conversation. "So we won the game?" he asked.

"That's right," I answered. "And we did it for you."

Billy's eyes got all watery.

"I'm sorry you weren't there," said Jamie, "but at least you can watch it on TV."

"Yeah," said Billy, "I can't wait to see it!"

We ordered enough food for a professional football team. Then we relived every wonderful minute of the game as we ate our lunch and watched the tape. I couldn't believe it! We had actually beaten the District 6 Champs, and I got to play center for the first time. I decided that this was probably the best day of my life.

CHAPTER FOURTEEN

Jimmy and I had a captive audience as we shared our Big Rapids experience with our friends in the cafeteria. Duffy and the rest of the hockey players listened intently as we described every exciting moment of the game.

"I can't believe how good your team has gotten!" remarked Duffy. "Don't you have any rookies?"

"Yeah," I answered. "We have three rookies and two of the smallest kids in the league. Our team is awesome — we have the best coach and the coolest jerseys."

Duffy rolled his eyes. "What do jerseys have to do with it?" he questioned.

"It's the Russian image," explained Jimmy, coming to my defense.

"And you know what else?" I added.

"What?" asked Duffy.

"All of the players have scored a goal except for one of the rookies."

"Well, if you guys can beat the District 6 Champs," remarked Duffy, "then you should be able to beat Rocky's."

"We'll find out on Saturday," said Jimmy, " 'cause that's when we play 'em."

The buzzer ended our lunchtime conversation, and I headed for English class.

"You should all enjoy your next assignment," announced Mr. Fisher as the students sighed and groaned. "I want you to write a two-page paper on your most exciting experience. It may be something that happened recently, or if you prefer, you may choose to write about an incident that occurred in your early childhood years. The assignment is due on Thursday. Any questions?"

I knew exactly what I'd be writing about. Up until last weekend, my life had been pretty boring. But what could be more exciting than beating the Big Rapids District 6 Champs? And with Mr. Fisher being the assistant coach, this was an automatic A!

I worked hard on my paper all week long. I think I could relive the moments of the Big Rapids game over and over again and never get tired of it. I handed my paper in on Thursday.

On Friday Mr. Fisher asked me to read my paper in front of the whole class. I usually hate reading assignments out loud, but this time it wasn't so bad.

"Great story!" exclaimed Mr. Fisher when I had finished. "And for those of you who think he might be exaggerating, he isn't. I know, because I was there."

I was glad my turn was over so I could sit down and relax while everyone else read their stories. Everyone roared as Jason Potts shared the story of how his swimsuit came off when he was waterskiing, and everyone groaned as Sharla Peters bragged about winning first place at her saxophone competition.

The week went by quickly, and we were on our way to practice again. I wished I could spend as much time at practice as I did at school. Boy, would I be good!

"Hey!" hollered Jimmy. "Turn up the radio!"

It was Sam the Sham and the Pharaohs singing "Louie, Louie." Jimmy and I sang along at the top of our lungs and made up a few of our own words as we sang.

"I see you're beginning to like my music," said Dad with a smile.

"Only that song," I replied. "It's Louie's theme song."

"Louie's a great player," my dad said. "You're lucky to have him on your team."

"Our goalie's not bad either," I remarked with a smirk.

"Thanks for the ride," said Jimmy as we climbed out of the van.

"You're welcome," answered Dad. "Have a good practice."

At practice, everyone was really pumped up for Saturday's game against Rocky's.

"Rocky's only lost one game," Coach Lou reminded us. "But they're no tougher than Big Rapids, so I think we have a good chance."

"They need to be humbled!" said Kurt. "And we're the ones who can do it!"

"Yeah," replied Mike, "we'll show those Wave

Runners that they belong in the water and not on the ice!"

"I don't want you guys to get an attitude against these kids," warned Coach Lou. "The coach is a friend of mine, and I want us to have a clean game. The reason they're in first place is that they're good. But we're good, too, and I think we can beat 'em. All I ask is that every player puts forth his best effort. Now go home and get to bed — we've got a big game tomorrow!"

I had a hard time sleeping. If we won the game, we'd still have a chance at being the league champions. I really hoped we would win. I also hoped that someday I'd be able to score a winning goal. Maybe that day would be soon . . .

At ten in the morning, the Dynamos were out on the ice ready to play. Coach Lou gave us an inspiring pep talk and said he expected great things for the game. When the referee dropped the puck, Rocky's Wave Runners won the face-off. They were quick to maneuver the puck to the Dynamo's net. Jimmy stopped three shots on goal before the Dynamos finally gained possession of the puck. We were really playing our best and giving it everything we had. But nothing seemed to work. Rocky's goalie was determined to keep the puck out of the net, which is exactly what he did. It was a scoreless game by the end of the first period, and both teams were equally frustrated.

"We're doing a great job of holdin' 'em," said Coach Lou, "but we need to score."

I got a little nervous when Louie asked to sit out

104

for a while. He said he wasn't feeling well and thought he might throw up. I knew that without Louie our chance of scoring was slim. A few minutes into the second period, Rocky's finally scored a goal, which gave them the edge they wanted.

The Dynamos didn't give up. We played hard and fast, but we just couldn't score a goal. At the end of the second period, Rocky's Wave Runners were leading one to nothing. I was relieved when Louie started feeling better and asked Coach to put him back in the game.

"Let's try to score!" shouted Coach Lou as we began the third period. "Show me what you can do!"

Kurt won the face-off and passed to Louie, who skated the puck straight to the net. I thought for sure he was going to score, but the puck hit the post and bounced back, giving Rocky's control. They held onto the puck for the next few minutes, but it seemed like hours. They finally broke through our defense, shooting the puck past Jimmy and into the net.

"Darn!" shouted Louie, who by now was getting very frustrated.

Meanwhile, Rocky's Wave Runners were celebrating as though they had already won the game.

"There's still plenty of time left," reminded Coach Lou as we gathered at the players bench. "Don't give up. I know you guys can do it!"

With a score of two to zero and three minutes left in the game, it'd be a pretty tall order to come back and win. I decided I'd be happy with a tie.

Denny and I went out on the ice to play wing.

Raw Meat and Mark were put on defense. Coach Lou decided to give Louie a rest and asked Benny to play center. Benny took his position with confidence, and when the puck hit the ice, his face-off pass went directly to Denny, who skated the puck toward the net. Then, before anyone knew what happened, Denny shot the puck into the net and scored.

The team went wild, and so did the fans, who were mostly our parents, of course. We all knew that Denny was the only Dynamo player who hadn't scored a goal, and everyone was hoping it would happen before the end of the season. Having him score a goal now caught everyone by surprise!

Those of us who were on the ice threw down our sticks and tossed our gloves in the air. The rest of the team jumped over the wall and mobbed Denny in front of the net.

"You need to finish the game!" shouted the ref as he interrupted our celebration.

After lots of hugs and high-fives, we finally picked up our sticks and gloves and went back to the bench. Coach Lou sent out a few fresh players to finish the game. As the minutes ticked away, I looked over at Denny and noticed tears running down his cheeks. I swallowed hard to fight back a few of my own. *Three, two, one* — the buzzer sounded and the game was over. Rocky's beat the Dynamos by a score of two to one. When we shook hands at the end of the game, one of Rocky's players asked me what the big deal was.

"Why are you guys so excited?" he asked. "You didn't win!"

"Everyone on our team has now scored a goal," I explained.

"So what?" he replied as he rolled his eyes.

"You'd have to be a Dynamo to understand," I answered.

When we all made it to the locker room, Jamie started chanting, "Speech, speech, speech!"

Denny knew this was his cue. He proudly and confidently took his stand on the bench and responded with a not so gentle "Whaaaat?" The entire locker room was in hysterics.

"Good job, Denny!" said Louie as he patted him on the back.

"Great goal," I said as I gave him a high-five.

One by one each player congratulated Denny. I figured this was probably the greatest moment of his life.

When Coach Lou read the stats, everyone cheered and shouted at the announcement of Alexi's first goal.

"I'm really happy for Alexi," continued Coach Lou. "It was a great goal. But unfortunately, with today's loss we don't have a shot at the title."

"Hey, Coach," I interrupted.

"Yes, Ivan," Coach Lou answered.

"Being a Dynamo is better than winning the championship title. I wouldn't trade places with any other team in the league — even Rocky's. At the beginning of the season, I was really hoping we could win the title, but that doesn't matter to me anymore. Rocky's might be in first place, but they don't have any idea what it's like to be a Dynamo."

"Being a Dynamo is the best!" agreed Jamie.

Then one by one, the players started chanting, "Dynamo, Dynamo, Dynamo," until we were all chanting in unison.

Coach Lou's eyes got all red and watery.

"The Dynamos are the best!" he said proudly. "And I've never had a better team!"

As we were getting ready to leave, I decided to congratulate Denny one more time.

"That was an awesome goal," I said.

"Thanks," answered Denny.

"So, Denny," I continued, "how come you just started playing hockey? You should have started years ago."

At first Denny just shrugged his shoulders, then he answered, "I didn't have any equipment, and my folks couldn't afford it. My grandparents gave it to me this year for a Christmas present."

The thought of not being able to afford equipment had never occurred to me. Then I thought about all the other kids who would love to play hockey, but would never play for that very reason. I realized then that I was pretty lucky.

CHAPTER FIFTEEN

There's something about Christmas morning that makes it impossible to sleep. I woke up at six thirty. I heard quiet footsteps in the hallway and discovered Chrissy snooping around.

"What ya doin'?" I whispered.

"Seein' if anyone's up," Chrissy answered.

"It's too early," I replied. "Go back to bed."

"I can't sleep," said Chrissy. "I'm too excited."

"Come into my room then," I invited.

Chrissy crawled into the spare bed that my friends use when they stay overnight. We talked quietly until seven o'clock.

"I can't take it anymore!" exclaimed Chrissy. "I'm going downstairs."

I decided it was worthless to stay in bed, since I'd never go back to sleep anyway. So I followed Chrissy into the family room.

"Look," said Chrissy, as she pointed to the bulging stockings on the mantle. "They're all filled."

"Yeah," I replied. "And it looks like Santa found the milk and cookies you left for him."

Chrissy picked up the empty mug from the hearth

and examined the small china plate which held only a few leftover cookie crumbs.

"Do you really think Santa drank the milk and ate the cookies?" asked Chrissy. "Or do you think that Dad does that?"

"I don't know," I replied. "What do you think?"

"Well," answered Chrissy, "Santa couldn't possibly eat cookies and drink milk at every house."

"Why not?" I asked.

"Because it would take too long," answered Chrissy. "And besides, no one could eat that much!"

"Maybe that's why he's so fat," I suggested.

"Oh, Andy," laughed Chrissy. "You're so silly!"

"Can't sleep?" asked Mom as she poked her head into the family room.

"Can we open presents now?" begged Chrissy.

"Not until James gets up," she answered.

"But what if he sleeps 'til noon?" Chrissy whined.

"If he's not up by eight, we'll wake him up, okay?"

"All right," agreed Chrissy with a sigh.

James finally woke up and joined us in the family room while my dad was busy setting up the video camera and unscrewing lamp shades so that everything would be perfect for the pictures. Sometimes he acted like a professional photographer, which totally annoyed the rest of us. But I had to admit that his videos and pictures usually turned out pretty well.

"Okay," announced Dad, "the camera is rolling. You may open your gifts."

Mom passed out several gifts in an attempt to establish some sort of order. But Chrissy's eagerness turned things into chaos, and soon wrapping paper was all over the family room floor.

"Oh, boy!" exclaimed Chrissy. "A new sleeping bag. I really need this for all my slumber parties. Thank you! Thank you!"

"Oh, I wonder what this is?" laughed James as he picked up a gift shaped like a tennis racquet.

"You get three guesses," said Dad, "and the first two don't count."

I opened some of my gifts, knowing I'd probably get clothes.

"Great jeans!" I said, relieved that my mom picked out the right brand. "And they're even the right size."

My next gift was a University of Michigan sweatshirt, which I liked a lot. But the last gift I opened was by far the best.

"Awesome jacket!" I exclaimed, as I gave my mom a hug.

It was the hockey jacket I had been hoping for. Most of the kids in the league had them, and of course, only hockey players wore them. The jacket was kelly green with gray fleece lining and had the league's initials printed across the back.

"Thanks Mom and Dad," I said. "I really wanted this jacket. And thanks for letting me play hockey. I know it costs a lot of money."

"We're just happy you've found something you enjoy doing," said Mom.

"You can keep the jacket if you keep playing hockey," teased Dad. "Otherwise, we're takin' it back."

"You won't have to take it back," I assured him. "'cause I'll be playin' hockey the rest of my life."

Then it was time for James, Chrissy, and me to pass out our gifts.

"Merry Christmas," I said to Mom and Dad as I gave them a present.

"Thanks, Andy," said Mom before she even opened it.

"Oh, wow!" exclaimed Dad as he pulled a wooden vase out of the box.

"I made it and stained it in shop," I explained. "You can use it for flowers or just leave it the way it is."

"It's beautiful," remarked Mom. "You did a great job."

"What did ya get me?" Chrissy asked eagerly.

"Here," said James. "It's from both of us."

Chrissy ripped open the paper. "A new gymnastics Barbie!" she squealed. "I love it! I love it!"

Then James and I handed each other gifts, knowing that they were probably the same thing.

"Nice T-shirt," I said as I opened the box. "My first Red Wings shirt. Thanks, James."

"I like mine, too," answered James, holding up a Nike tennis shirt. "Thanks, Andy."

"You're welcome," I answered.

As Mom was picking up wads of wrapping paper, I gathered my gifts and brought them to my room.

"Hey," said James, "maybe you'll get some patches to put on your jacket."

"Yeah," I answered, "if I ever earn any."

"With the way you've been playin'," James continued, "you'll be earning lots of 'em."

"Time to eat!" Mom called from the kitchen.

We sat down to our traditional candlelight Christmas breakfast in the dining room. But before we could indulge, we had to sit quietly as Dad opened the Bible and read the Christmas story from the second chapter of Luke, reminding us of the real meaning of Christmas. After Dad gave thanks for the food, I sunk my teeth into the center of a hot cinnamon roll that was begging to be devoured. I ate three pieces of Polish sausage and a spoonful of cheese soufflé so Mom would see that I at least tried it.

When breakfast was over and the dishes were done, we drove to Middleville to spend the rest of the day with my mom's family. James and I have some girl cousins who are fun to be with. We had a two hour Ping-Pong tournament — boys against girls. We played so many games, we lost count of who won the most.

Then we opened presents. The cousins draw names every year, and we never know who has our name until we get our gift.

"Hey," I said to my cousin Mary. "I had your name, and you had mine."

"I hope you got me something good," she teased.

"I always give good gifts," I replied.

Mary gave me a leather wallet, and I gave her a pair of maroon-and-white soccer shorts 'cause those are her school's colors and she loves to play soccer.

My grandpa and grandma always give us a card with money in it, and every year my grandpa says the same thing: "If it's too big you can return it." Of course everyone always laughs.

Then we had to eat again, even though I wasn't hungry. After we ate dinner, it was time to go home, and I was kind of sad that Christmas was over.

• • •

Coach Lou decided to take advantage of our week off from school. He had us practice every chance we could get. When we couldn't play at the ice rink, we practiced on outdoor ponds and gymnasium floors. Coach Lou wanted us to be in good shape for the play-offs, which were only a few weeks away.

Jamie's dad got some tickets to a semi-pro hockey game, and on Thursday night, the whole Dynamo team plus the coaches and a few parents drove to Muskegon to watch the Lumberjacks and the Panthers play hockey. Because we were all wearing our Dynamo jerseys, we got a lot of stares from the people in the bleachers.

"Where you guys from?" asked a curious fan sitting behind us.

"We're exchange students from Russia," answered Jamie as the rest of us tried not to laugh. "And we all play hockey."

"I'll bet you guys are good," commented the fan.

"Yes, we are," agreed Jamie.

The game finally started, and we were all impressed with how fast the players could skate.

"We'll be able to play that well some day," Mike said confidently.

"Only if we play every day for the rest of our lives," added Louie.

The Lumberjacks scored two goals in the first period, while the Panthers scored one.

"It's been a pretty clean game so far," commented Coach Lou during the break. "Sometimes these games can get rough."

As songs from the sixties were being blasted over the sound system, Jamie, Mike, and I started clapping and swaying to the music. Soon the entire audience joined in. Everything was pretty much under control until "Louie, Louie" sounded its way through the monitors.

"This is our song!" I shouted.

With that announcement, we all stood up on the bleachers and began dancing and singing along with Sam the Sham and the Pharaohs. Coach Lou and Mr. Fisher were laughing hysterically as the entire audience was being entertained by the singing Dynamos. When the song was finally over, the crowd clapped and cheered louder than they had at any time during the game.

"Whew!" exclaimed Coach Lou. "I'm glad that's over!"

"Coach," I said, "we couldn't resist."

"That's okay." replied Coach Lou. "But it's time to calm down."

We took our seats as the second period began. The Lumberjacks won the face-off, but the Panthers quickly took the puck away and went for a goal. The puck hit the goalie in the head and knocked him down.

"Now I know why we wear helmets," remarked Jimmy.

"Yeah," added Billy, "if that guy wasn't wearing a helmet, he'd be dead."

"No kidding," said Jamie. "Or maybe he'd need a head transplant."

"There's no such thing as a head transplant," stated Louie. "The patient would bleed to death while his head was off."

"Let's not talk about this while I'm eating," begged Kurt.

"You're always eating," replied Jamie.

"I don't eat half as much as you do!" defended Kurt.

"Hey, let's watch the game," instructed Louie.

There were no goals scored in the second period, but we witnessed the biggest brawl any of us had ever seen. Three of the Lumberjacks were given major penalties, and one of the Panthers was suspended. It took five minutes for the players and refs to gather up the sticks and gloves that were scattered all over the ice.

During the next intermission, we went to the concession to stock up on food supplies for the third period. When we returned to our seats, an announcement came over the loud speaker: "At this time we would like to declare the winner of the six-foot submarine sandwich we give away every Thursday night to the most enthusiastic fan. We have decided that tonight's sub sandwich goes to the Dynamo hockey team from Grand City!"

116

With that announcement, the Dynamos went wild, and we all started dancing and cheering and making complete fools of ourselves.

"I thought you guys were from Russia," remarked one of the fans who was sitting behind Jamie.

"Uh," Jamie hesitated, "well, we used to be from Russia, but we're adopted."

"Nice try, kid!" answered the fan with a laugh. "You had me fooled for a while."

Jamie heaved a sigh of relief and was glad the guy took the whole thing as a joke.

The third period went by quickly, and the Lumberjacks won the game four to two.

"Stay here," instructed Coach Lou. "I'm going to get the coupon for the sub."

The Dynamos stayed in their seats, and soon Coach Lou returned with the coupon in hand.

"This is only good at the Sub Shop in Muskegon," said Coach Lou, "so we might as well stop there on the way home."

We all thought it was a great idea and decided to meet at the Sub Shop on Second Avenue. It's a good thing we weren't very hungry, because by the time everyone got a slice of the sub sandwich, there wasn't much left. I finally got home at one-thirty in the morning. I had definitely decided there was nothing more fun than being with Coach Lou and the Dynamos.

CHAPTER SIXTEEN

In the following weeks, the Dynamos won four out of five games. We went into the play-offs with an impressive record of twenty-three wins, nine losses, and two ties. Rocky's Wave Runners were in first place, but the runner-up title was still undecided. If the Dynamos did well in the play-offs, we had a chance at runner-up and could even get a trophy. I wanted badly for Coach Lou to get a trophy, 'cause if any coach deserved one, he did.

Our first game in the play-offs was against De Young's Furniture. We had an easy win with a score of five to one. In our next game, we barely squeaked by Ben's Auto, four to three. Then we tied Tony's Pizza three to three, and finally we were up against Rocky's for the final game of the season. If we beat Rocky's, we would finish the season in second place.

When I walked into the locker room, I was surprised to see red-and-white hearts on the bench and wondered what on earth Coach Lou was up to.

"Uh, Coach," I asked, "are these hearts leftover from a Valentine's Day party or something?"

"Those are ours, Ivan," answered Coach Lou. "I've decided that since it's Valentine's Day and the last game of the season, we should send a love message to your moms. If you guys hold them up in the right order they spell, *WE LOVE YOU MOM.*"

"But Coach," I protested, "won't Rocky's think we're a bunch of sissies?"

"Not if we kick their butts," replied Coach Lou.

I couldn't believe it! Coach Lou had some pretty unique ideas, but this was one idea I wasn't too sure of.

"There's no way I'm holding up any heart!" protested Kurt.

"Me either!" agreed Jamie. "This is sissy stuff!"

"You will if you want to play," answered Coach Lou. "Your moms make a lot of sacrifices so you guys can play hockey. This will be a great surprise for them as well as a way of saying thank you. There are twelve letters, one for each player. Make sure you sit in the right order so that the message is spelled correctly."

Mike and Jamie started mixing up the letters to see what other words they could spell.

"How about MOO YOU?" asked Jamie.

"Oh, that makes a lot of sense," replied Mike.

"Excuse me, people," interrupted Coach Lou, "but we have a game to play. And, by the way, the coach from Oakwood called and asked if we wanted to play them next week for a post-season game. He feels bad about what happened in our game against them and wants a chance to make things right. The player that hurt Louie has been suspended for the rest of the year, and the coach promised me a clean game. It'd be our last chance to play together as a team. What do you say?"

"I say let's play," said Jimmy

"Me, too," agreed Benny and Louie.

The rest of us agreed, and I was glad that we would have one more chance to play together, even if it was against Oakwood.

"It's settled then," said Coach Lou. "Friday night we'll have our awards' banquet, and Saturday morning we'll play Oakwood on their ice. But now we have to play Rocky's — so let's get out there and do what we need to do! Ivan, take us out to the ice."

I led the team in the rap, and then we headed for the ice. We each had our valentine with the appropriate letter, and we sat on the players bench in the correct order. With a nod from Coach Lou, we held up our message for all the moms in the bleachers. No one knew if it was intentional or not, but Raw Meat, who was holding the letter W, held it upside down so the message read *ME LOVE YOU MOM*.

The Dynamo fans laughed, applauded, and cheered while the Wave Runners stared at us in disbelief.

With that out of the way, we were ready to play. Benny, Kurt, Ricky, Mark, and Jamie were sent out to start the game. Benny won the face-off for the Dynamos and passed to Mark, who took the puck into Wave Runner territory. In the first few minutes the puck went back and forth, then Kurt broke through the defense and scored a goal for the Dynamos.

"Good job, Vladimir!" shouted Coach Lou.

I could tell that Coach Lou really wanted to win this game, just to prove that we could beat the number one team. A few minutes later, Louie scored a goal, which gave us some added confidence. Jimmy was having one of his greatest games of the season and kept Rocky's from scoring until late in the first period.

We went into the second period with a two to one lead.

"If I can score one more goal," Louie said to me on the bench, "I will have fifty goals this season."

"So make it happen," I responded. "You can do it."

Louie and I went out on the ice with Billy and the micro defense. We passed the puck back and forth and occasionally lost it to Rocky's offensive players. Rocky's had several shots on goal, but they couldn't get the puck past Jimmy.

"You guys are playing an outstanding game," Coach Lou exclaimed during a brief time-out. "Keep doing what you're doing and don't let them score!"

I watched from the bench as Kurt and Benny kept control of the puck during the last two minutes of the second period. With ten seconds left, Kurt scored another goal for the Dynamos, giving us a three to one lead.

"Congratulations Vladimir!" announced Coach Lou during the break. "That was your twenty-fifth goal for the season."

"Oh, cool," responded Kurt, trying to be modest as everyone patted him on the back.

"I can't believe what's happening here," exclaimed Coach Lou.

"We're scoring, and they're not!" Mike explained simply.

"That's right," added Coach Lou. "Just keep it up for one more period!"

Rocky's scored another goal in the first few minutes of the third period, which kept us ahead by only one goal. Things were getting rather tense until Louie maneuvered a perfect breakaway and scored again for the Dynamos. I skated straight for Louie and gave him such a big hug that we both fell down.

"I knew you could do it!" I hollered as we picked ourselves up.

Louie smiled and nodded.

"We've gotta beat these guys," he said.

"We will," I assured him. "We need to do it for your dad."

"There's still plenty of time," Coach Lou reminded us during a brief break. "Try not to get over-confident — and whatever you do, don't let them score!"

My heart began to pound as I watched the minutes tick away and thought about the possibility of beating Rocky's. I couldn't think of a better way to end the season than by beating the number one team. With only one minute left in the game, Louie passed to Billy in front of the net. Billy shot and scored. My wish came true as the buzzer sounded and the Dynamos beat Rocky's five to two. We cried and cheered and mobbed each other on the ice. But the refs broke up our celebration so they could get on with the pre-sentation of the trophies. Tears rolled down my cheeks as Coach Lou proudly received the runner-up trophy.

"All I can say," responded Coach Lou, "is that it's been a privilege to coach such a great bunch of kids! This trophy is for them, and I couldn't be prouder!"

Coach Lou held up the trophy as everyone clapped, whistled, and cheered. The Dynamos were good sports as we watched Rocky's Wave Runners receive the first place trophy.

As we skated off the ice toward the locker room, I was surprised when the captain of Rocky's came over to me.

"Hey, Ivan," called the captain.

"Yeah?" I answered.

"Your team is all right," he exclaimed.

"Thanks," I replied. "So is yours."

When I went into the locker room and realized that our season was officially over, I was glad we still had one more game to play. I wished that the season didn't have to end. I wished I could be a Dynamo every year and our team could always stay together.

"Read us the stats!" shouted Raw Meat at the top of his lungs.

"With pleasure!" answered Coach Lou. "You guys did it! You actually beat the number one team. This is unbelievable! Here's what happened: Sergei had a great game with ten passes, nine take-aways, and one assist. Ivan had eight passes, seven take-aways, and no penalties."

"Yea, Ivan!" interrupted Jamie.

"Petr and Nikolai," continued Coach Lou, "our awesome micro defense team, kept the puck in our offensive zone more than any other game this season. Raw Meat Igor stole the puck eleven times — twice in front of Rocky's net, which kept them from scoring. Vladimir scored his twenty-fifth goal for the season, and Chevy scored his fiftieth."

With that announcement the entire locker room erupted into a chorus of shouts and cheers, while Kurt and Louie gave each other a high-five.

"Tell us more!" begged Mark when things finally calmed down.

"Well, Victor," replied Coach Lou, "you had an outstanding game with nine blocks, eight passes, and seven take-aways. Boris had four shots on goal, six passes, and eight blocks. Mikail took the puck away from our opponents seven times and scored the last goal of the game. Alexi played his heart out with six blocks, seven take-aways, and three shots on goal, and Tretyak kept Rocky's from scoring fifteen times. What more can I say? You guys are incredible!"

"I say we do the rap," suggested Jamie. "Take it away, Ivan!"

Yo! We're the Dynamos and we're here to say,
When we come to the rink, we come to play.

This time, even the coaches and Mr. Jones joined the Dynamos in reciting the rap. When Mr. Jones got up on the bench and started dancing, we all laughed so hard we couldn't even finish the rap.

124

"What's goin' on in here?" inquired my dad as he stuck his head in the locker room.

"A little post-game craziness," answered Coach Lou.

"Well," Dad continued, "you'll be even more crazy when you find out your parents left 'cause they got tired of waiting for you."

"Ivan's dad is right," agreed Coach Lou. "You guys need to get out of here. I'll see you Friday night."

With that announcement, we all gathered up our stuff and made a quick exit out of the locker room.

CHAPTER SEVENTEEN

I was glad that the awards' banquet wasn't being held at a fancy restaurant where we'd have to get all dressed up and eat a formal dinner with three forks, two knives, and too many spoons. Coach Lou knew what we liked. He decided to have the party at a bowling alley with lots of pop, junk food, and pepperoni pizza.

One by one, the Dynamos arrived at Pete's Pins wearing their blue jeans and yellow jerseys. Most of the parents, brothers, and sisters came as well. Denny even brought his grandparents. Everyone had a great time trying to bowl. A few of the Dynamos knew what they were doing, but most of us didn't even know how to keep score.

I bowled in a lane with Mike, Freddie, and Billy.

"Oh, no!" I cried as I watched the heavy black ball fall into the gutter for the third time.

"What you moanin' about?" asked Billy. "You've knocked down the most pins so far."

"Hey," said Mike, "this is the first time I've ever bowled."

"Me, too," added Freddie.

"It's a good thing you guys are hockey players,"

remarked Coach Lou, " 'cause you sure are pathetic at bowling!"

"How come *you're* not bowling?" Mike asked him.

"The lanes are full," answered Coach Lou. "Besides, I don't want you laughin' at me."

"Time to eat!" shouted Mrs. Jones.

With that announcement, we dropped our bowling balls and ran into the party room, which some of the moms had decorated. There were yellow-and-black balloons and streamers everywhere. Mark's mom had made Dynamo jerseys out of construction paper and strung them across the room. There was one for every player — complete with Russian name and Dynamo number.

"Help yourselves to the pizza," announced Coach Lou. "And before we hand out the awards, we're going to have a little slide show that Alexi's dad put together for us."

After grabbing two pieces of pizza, I sat on the floor next to Louie and waited for the slide show to begin.

"There's Billy and Kurt," Jamie yelled when the first picture appeared on the screen.

"And there's Ivan goin' in for a goal," added Coach Lou as the slide show continued.

It was really neat seeing all of us in action and reliving some of our favorite moments. The background music added to the mood, and we all joined in singing "We will we will rock you" as it blasted through the speakers.

"Here's the sub sandwich you guys won," said Denny's dad, as he showed us the picture of everyone at the restaurant. "And here's the final shot."

Everyone clapped and cheered at the close up of Coach Lou holding the runner-up trophy high above his head.

With the slide show over, the presentations began. Coach Lou, Mr. Fisher, and Mr. Jones went to the front of the room with a box full of trophies and certificates.

"I would like to begin," announced Mr. Fisher, "by acknowledging Jimmy 'Tretyak' Cleaver, our awesome goalie."

As Jimmy got up to receive his award the parents all shouted, "Holy, moly what a goalie!" which is what they shouted at every game whenever Jimmy would make a remarkable save.

"And what a goalie he is!" exclaimed Mr. Fisher. "Not only did Tretyak receive television coverage, but he was also selected as 'Goalie of the Year' by the Grand City Amateur Hockey Association. Tretyak was always calm under pressure and played a major role in all of our wins. He made four hundred twenty-nine saves this season and achieved six shutouts. Congratulations, Tretyak!"

Everyone applauded as Jimmy gratefully accepted his trophy and certificates.

"Next on the list," continued Mr. Fisher, "I'd like to acknowledge Benny 'Sergei' Baker."

Benny stood by Mr. Fisher and blushed as the presentation was made.

"Sergei usually played center, but was ready and

willing to play wherever the coaches needed him. He was often called on to penalty kill and was always there to catch a puck on rebound and send it back into the net for a goal. Sergei, I'd like to present this trophy to you."

"Thank you," he replied modestly. "I really enjoyed being on this awesome team."

"The next Dynamo that I'd like to recognize," said Mr. Fisher, "is Ricky 'Raw Meat Igor' Clay. Ricky would you please come forward?"

Ricky smiled and nodded as he made his way to the front of the room.

"Igor was a rookie who played like a veteran," commented Mr. Fisher. "He was tough and aggressive and was a real defensive force in the Dynamo zone. He blocked shots, took away the puck from opposing players, and often sacrificed his body in the process. Igor, please accept the trophy you earned."

"Thanks," replied Ricky. "I can't wait 'til next year when body checking is legal!"

The Dynamos clapped as Ricky took his seat, and Kurt went forward to be the next one in the spotlight.

"Kurt 'Vladimir' Hall," announced Mr. Fisher, "established himself as a dangerous goal scorer. He not only earned a hat trick for himself, but also helped Chevy get a playmaker. He had an eight-game scoring streak and scored a game-winning goal against De Young's Furniture. Congratulations Vladimir on a great season."

"I'd like to thank all of my coaches," replied Kurt.

"And especially my mom and dad for hauling me to all the games and practices."

As Mr. Fisher and Kurt went back to their seats, Coach Lou stood up and asked Mike Hanson to come forward.

"Mike 'Petr' Hanson is better known as part of our micro defense," announced Coach Lou. "His small stature was compensated for with his big heart and fast legs. He could outskate any opponent, and his defensive skills kept the puck out of the Dynamo net. Petr, I'm pleased to present you with this beautiful trophy."

"Hey, thanks!" replied Mike. "It was fun being a Dynamo. I especially like the time when my dad yelled at the ref for giving me a penalty."

Everyone burst out laughing as Mike took a bow and went back to his seat.

"The other half of our micro defense," Coach Lou continued, "is Freddie 'Nikolai' Rogers. Nikolai scored his first goal of the season in his first game, shortly after having his tonsils out. We all knew then that he'd be a great asset to our team. Nikolai, what did you enjoy most about this season?"

"Beating the London team," Feddie answered without hesitation as Coach Lou handed him his trophy and everyone clapped.

"Would Jamie 'Boris Doris' Jones please come forward?" Coach Lou requested as we all laughed. "Boris never had a bad game. He always played his best and was one of our strongest defensive players. He could play wherever the team needed him and always kept his eye on the puck. Boris, what was the best experience for you this season?"

"Well," replied Jamie as he thought for a moment. "I think the best thing was that everyone on the team scored a goal."

With that comment Coach Lou got pretty choked up and had a hard time talking.

"Mark 'Victor' Olson is the next to be honored," Coach Lou continued as he cleared his throat. "Victor led the team in takes-aways and was never afraid to fight for the puck. He developed into a strong player and could play every position with skill. Victor, I'm proud to present you with this trophy and hope that it will always remind you of this season."

"Thanks a lot!" said Mark as he took his trophy and went back to his seat.

Coach Lou paused for a minute, then he took a deep breath. "I've been dreading this day," he admitted as tears swelled up in his eyes, "because I don't want this season to end. I've coached a lot of teams, and this is the greatest bunch of kids I've ever had. But, hey, let's finish the awards. Louie 'Vyacheslav' Richards. You're on!"

"Go, Louie!" shouted Jamie as Louie stepped forward.

"Chevy was our leading scorer," said Coach Lou, "with a remarkable fifty goals. He had twenty-nine assists, nine hat tricks, and eleven game-winning goals. He played both forward and defense and could score from anywhere on the ice. I'm proud to say that Chevy was an unselfish player and many times tried

131

to help his teammates score. Chevy always gave a hundred percent and knew how to frustrate the opponent. Chevy, congratulations on an outstanding season."

"Thanks, Dad," said Louie as he accepted the trophy. "I've been playing hockey a lot of years and this was by far my favorite." Louie's voice quivered as he added, "I'm gonna miss being a Dynamo."

By now the room was really quiet, and even the parents started sniffing and blowing their noses. I started to get nervous and wondered when I'd be up.

"Billy 'Mikail' Peterson," said Coach Lou, "please come forward to receive your award."

Billy got up and stood next to Coach Lou as Coach Lou made the next presentation.

"Billy was an inspiration to all of us," he said. "With determination and hard work, he developed into a skilled player. He played both defense and forward and took the puck away from the opponent almost every time he was on the ice. He was a team player and a good example. Billy, I hope you consider playing more hockey and less baseball in the coming year."

Billy laughed as he took the trophy from Coach Lou.

"Well, I don't think I'll ever stop playing baseball," he said, "but I am going to practice hockey a lot."

As Billy went back to his seat, Coach Lou asked Denny to come forward.

"Denny 'Alexi' Smith," stated Coach Lou, "may have been a quiet kid in the locker room, but he was an animal on the ice. He was one of our fastest skaters who made a lot of progress throughout the season. The Dynamos will always remember his goal against Rocky's as one of the highlights of our season. Denny, you had a great season, is there anything you'd like to say?"

"I just wanna thank my grandparents," he said, "for giving me my equipment so I could play."

As Denny was going back to his seat, Jamie shouted, "Speech, speech, speech."

Denny answered, "Whaaaat?" and all the Dynamos burst out laughing.

Then my heart started pounding because I knew I was the last one to get a trophy.

"Ivan," said Coach Lou, "come on up."

The room got quiet as I went forward.

"The best thing that happened to our team," Coach Lou announced as he put his arm across my shoulders, "is that Andy 'Ivan' Anderson got traded. Our team wouldn't have been the same without him."

Coach Lou started sniffing again, and I saw a tear roll down his cheek when he blinked. I tried hard not to cry.

"He was our leader both on and off the ice," Coach Lou continued as he wiped his eyes. "He knew how to make practices fun, he entertained us in the locker room, and he inspired us on the ice. The first time he played center, he played it like a pro and led us to victory against the District 6 Champs. Ivan's hard work paid off — and I was proud to have him on our team."

Tears burned in my eyes as Coach Lou handed me the trophy. I swallowed hard and tried to talk. "I'm gonna keep playin' hockey," I said as I took a deep breath, "but I know I'll probably never be on a team like this one."

At that moment I didn't care what anyone thought. I gave Coach Lou a hug and started to cry. The room was so quiet you could have heard an ant crawling across the floor. It seemed as though no one knew what to do next.

Finally, Mr. Fisher stood up and announced, "I think the bowling alley is closing. If we don't clear out of here, we'll be spending the night."

With that comment the Dynamos cheered with excitement and begged their parents to let them stay.

"We're not spending the night," insisted Mr. Jones. "We have a game to play tomorrow. Besides, the food's all gone, so you'd starve by tomorrow morning."

The parents agreed that it was time to go home, and the Dynamos parted with everyone saying, "See ya tomorrow."

CHAPTER EIGHTEEN

The next morning the locker room was quiet. Conversation was awkward and forced. A few of the players tried to make jokes, but nobody laughed. Coach Lou knew it was time for a pep talk.

"I think we're pretty lucky to be able to play one more game together," he reminded us. "Let's play this game like we played all of our other games. We're gonna play as a team, we'll give it all we got, and we're gonna play to win. Do you understand?"

"Yeah, Coach," I answered, "we get it."

Just then Benny's mom knocked on the locker room door. She handed Coach Lou a box of pucks. "May I come in?" she asked.

"Coast is clear," Coach Lou answered. "We're all dressed."

"I thought you guys might like something to help you remember this season," she said.

We all gathered around her as she showed us the pucks.

"Every player has a puck with his name on it and the number of goals he scored this season," she explained.

"Wow!" exclaimed Mike, "these are really cool!"

"Did you make these?" asked Jamie.

"Yes, she did," answered Coach Lou. "How about a Dynamo thank you?"

"Thank you Mrs. Baker," the Dynamos answered in unison as if it had been rehearsed.

"You're very welcome," replied Benny's mom. "I hope you enjoy them."

As Mrs. Baker left the locker room, I brought my puck over to Coach Lou.

"Nice puck," said Coach Lou.

"Yeah," I agreed with a smile, "but there's a mistake on mine. It says nine goals, but I'm gonna score today so it should say ten."

"The only way you can predict the future," Coach Lou replied, "is to make it happen."

"Well," I answered, "I'm gonna make it happen."

"It's time to play hockey," announced Mr. Fisher as he stuck his head in the locker room. "The Oakwood boys are waiting for you."

With that announcement, we quickly grabbed our sticks and left the locker room chanting the Dynamo rap with grand enthusiasm. We skated a few laps, shot some pucks, and got in position for the opening face-off.

The first period went by so quickly it seemed like a mistake when the buzzer sounded. There were no penalties and no goals, only a lot of skating and passing the puck back and forth across the ice.

In the middle of the second period, Louie finally scored a goal, but in a matter of minutes, Oakwood tied the game. There were no more goals in the second period, so the third period began with a one-one tie.

"You guys can do it!" exclaimed Coach Lou. "You're really outplayin' them — you just need another goal."

In the third period, Oakwood was more aggressive. They kept the game in the Dynamo zone and had several shots on goal. Raw Meat and Jamie were tough on defense, and Jimmy stopped everything that came his way. But if we were going to score, we needed to do it soon. With only two minutes left in the game, Louie finally got control of the puck and brought it into Oakwood's territory. He took a shot, but the puck rebounded off the goalie's skate and was picked up by an Oakwood player. For some reason, at that particular moment, I had more energy than I'd ever felt in my life. I caught up with the Oakwood guy and slid the end of my stick between his stick and the puck. Then I skated the puck in front of the net and sent it sailing through the goalie's legs for a Dynamo goal.

"Yes, Ivan!" I heard Coach Lou scream so loudly that I thought he was standing right next to me.

With only nine seconds on the clock, my teammates went wild! The guys from the bench mobbed the rest of us on the ice. Everyone was cheering, hugging, and crying, "Way to go, Ivan!" all at the same time.

The refs finally broke up our party and insisted that we play the remaining seconds of the game. Coach Lou put me at center. I won the face-off and passed the puck to Louie, who skated it toward the Oakwood net. *Three, two, one.* The buzzer sounded, the game was over, and I realized that my dream had come true. I had scored the winning goal for the Dynamos.

After we shook hands with Oakwood, Louie and Kurt picked me up and put me on their shoulders. The rest of the Dynamos gathered around us and we skated off the ice as a team. But once we entered the locker room, the joy of victory was replaced by the sobering thought that we had finally come to the end. Slowly and quietly we took off our jerseys and equipment and put on our clothes. Nobody talked. Nobody teased. Nobody laughed. The only sound that was heard was the zipping of hockey bags.

Mr. Jones opened the door and came in the locker room.

"Hey, you guys," he said ignoring the silence, "we're havin' a Dynamo reunion this summer at our house. It's June tenth, and you better all be there."

Knowing that we'd be together again made our final good-bye a little easier.

Coach Lou stood by the door as the players began to leave. Kurt, Mark, and Benny, were the first ones to leave.

"Good luck, you guys," said Coach Lou as he gave them each a high-five.

"See ya Coach," answered Kurt.

Then Denny, Billy, and Raw Meat headed for the door.

"You won't be rookies next year," said Coach Lou. "You'll be awesome."

They smiled and nodded their heads as they left.

Freddie and Mike were the next to leave.

"The micro defense!" Coach Lou exclaimed. "You'll probably both grow a foot by next fall."

"I hope so," said Mike.

"Me, too," added Freddie.

"Holy, moly, it's the goalie!" said Coach Lou as Jimmy walked past.

Jimmy laughed a little and said, "Thanks for everything, Coach."

Mr. Jones, Jamie, Louie, and I were the only ones left besides Coach Lou. I got up from the bench and slowly walked toward the door.

"You made it happen," Coach Lou said softly as he wrapped his arms around me.

I nodded my head in agreement. Then with tears streaming down my face I looked into his eyes, whispered "Thanks," and left the locker room.

Mr. Jones followed me into the lobby, "Great season, Ivan," he said as he patted me on the back.

"It sure was," I replied as I sniffed and wiped my face. "Hey, what shall I bring to your party?"

"How about a six-foot sub?" he suggested.

"Okay," I replied. "I'll try to win another one."

Then I noticed my parents, who were patiently waiting for me in the lobby.

"Ready to go, son?" asked my dad.

"Yeah, Dad," I answered, "I'm ready."

On the way home I stared out the window and watched the cars going in the opposite direction. I wanted to thank my mom and dad for making me play hockey again this year. I wanted to tell them that I liked going to North Middle and that they always seemed to know what was best for me. But it's hard for a kid to say those things.

"Thanks for everything," I managed to say.

Mom and Dad smiled and nodded their heads. They knew what I meant.